GUARDIAN OF THE TOMB

E.COOMBE

GUARDIAN OF THE TOMB

ARKY STEELE

A Lothian Children's Book

Published in Australia and New Zealand in 2013
by Hachette Australia
(an imprint of Hachette Australia Pty Limited)
Level 17, 207 Kent Street, Sydney NSW 2000
www.hachettechildrens.com.au

10 9 8 7 6 5 4 3 2

National Library of Australia
Cataloguing-in-Publication data:

Coombe, E.
Guardian of the tomb / E. Coombe
Arky Steele 1

978 0 7344 1158 7 (pbk.)

Genghis Khan, 1162-1227 – Juvenille fiction.
Archaeology – Mongolia – Juvenile fiction.

A823.4

Cover design by Xou Creative
Text design by Bookhouse, Sydney
Typeset in 12.75/20 pt Garamond Premier Pro
Printed and bound in Australia by McPherson's Printing Group

MIX
Paper from
responsible sources
FSC
www.fsc.org   FSC® C001695

The paper this book is printed on is certified against the
Forest Stewardship Council® Standards. McPherson's Printing
Group holds FSC® chain of custody certification SA-COC-005379.
FSC® promotes environmentally responsible, socially beneficial
and economically viable management of the world's forests.

To Jude

Prologue

I am the Keeper of Secrets. Tomorrow my head will be sliced from my neck and placed upon my knees. I must die to keep the Khan's tomb and treasure safe.

Together with one hundred footmen, fifty soldiers and fifty of Genghis Khan's guards, I took his vast treasure from the palace and went to the wild peaks.

When we were far from humanity, we made camp. The next day, leaving the guards behind, we went deeper into the mountains with the footmen and the soldiers carrying the treasure.

Once the treasure was hidden, the soldiers slaughtered the footmen. When we returned to camp, the waiting guards murdered the soldiers. We hid the soldiers' bodies so that even their ghosts would keep the secret.

I built his tomb to his orders. I killed all who worked on it and buried them in a vast unmarked grave.

When the great Khan died, I escorted him to his secret tomb, with a guard of 999 soldiers, and placed him in his golden coffin. I poisoned the soldiers so they lie with my master, protecting him for all eternity.

I locked the hidden tomb door, taking the three-part key with me.

At the Khan's order, I prepared clues and objects, riddles and hidden places, to lead a clever man to the treasure. To find the treasure, you must first find the tomb.

The Book of Clues will lead the way. The book is hidden well, yet easy to find.

To find the key to the hidden tomb, you will have to know that death holds the key. A gold coin is the first part of the key.

I will be the first to smile upon the key hunter.

The Dragon with a Pearl in its Mouth

Arky's mum was packing her climbing equipment when he came home from school. 'Are you off *again*?' he asked, grabbing hold of an ice-pick.

'Yep.' His mum smiled. 'Alaska—to one of the world's deadliest mountains.'

Arky wasn't surprised. His mum, Alice Steele, was considered one of the world's top mountaineers. Her bright blue eyes and pretty face sold climbing equipment. Sports stores all over the world sponsored her to make documentaries about her adventures.

'Got to fly out next week, and I'll be gone for most of your holidays, but your dad's got some news.'

'Where is he?'

Arky's question was answered as Doc bounced through the front door carrying a box. Alice looked up from her packing as Doc plonked himself down beside her.

'Lord Wright gave me this,' he said, opening the box.

Inside was a big gold coin. Arky leant over to see it better, so Doc picked it up and pressed it into Arky's hand. Arky rolled it in his palm. It was heavy and had a dragon's head on one side and strange designs on the other.

'What does it mean?' he said.

'The dragon with a pearl in its mouth means wisdom and power.' Doc turned the coin over in Arky's palm. 'On the back it says, "the first to death, glory and gold". It's the sign of Genghis Khan.'

'Who's he?' Arky asked.

Doc launched into a story. 'Genghis Khan was a cruel and violent man. By the time he was twenty-one, he was king of a great Mongolian empire. He robbed towns and filled his treasure houses with stolen loot. But when he died, his treasure vanished!'

'How come?'

'Genghis had many sons from lots of wives.' Alice picked up the story. 'He knew his sons would kill each other for his wealth. He didn't want his treasure wasted by war and fighting, so he hid it from his family.'

'I was hunting for his tomb several years ago,' Doc said. 'It was where I first met your mum.' He put his arm affectionately around Alice's slender waist. 'My team and I spent months searching for the tomb in the Himalayas, but thieves made our lives miserable, following us and taking our things. Eventually the weather turned bad and our funding was cut.'

'I was climbing up in the Himalayas then,' Alice said, 'doing my first extreme action documentary. The first snows arrived early and we met in an icy town. Your dad looked so sad to be leaving his dream behind. Then he saw me and cheered up.'

She gave Doc a kiss on the cheek. 'Oh, it was *so* romantic! Stuck in a wild snowstorm . . .'

'Yuck!' blurted Arky, to stop his parents getting soppy. 'Why's this coin so important?'

'While I was in Mongolia, I found an old manuscript written by someone who claimed to be the Keeper of Secrets—Genghis Khan's right-hand man. The manuscript told of a key that will open the door of Genghis's tomb. It also mentioned a gold coin. But the manuscript was so old that it almost fell to dust when I unrolled it.'

'But we believe the manuscript held real clues,' Alice said, 'and now this coin has turned up, which proves it.'

'Where's the manuscript now?' Arky was impressed by the story. He studied the designs on the coin again and wondered what other mysteries a keeper of secrets would know about.

'What's left of the manuscript is in a Mongolian library, but I've got a translation locked in my desk.' Doc smiled. 'You can read it later.'

'And how did Lord Wright get hold of this coin?' Arky asked.

'A shepherd boy found it, way out in the high plains in Mongolia,' Doc replied. 'No one's allowed to take old things out of countries, but sadly it happens. The shepherd boy would have sold this coin in the markets in good faith, but then it was sold on by criminals. Lord Wright thought it was probably a fake. When I told him it was real, he contacted the Mongolian government.'

'Is he returning it?' asked Alice.

'He will,' said Doc. 'But first, he tracked down the shepherd boy because he knows how much I'd love to find out more. So, while you're climbing your mountains, Arky and I are going to Mongolia.'

'*I'm* going?' cried Arky, his blue eyes sparkling.

'You're fit and strong like your mum,' Doc said, smiling. 'And the best at the rock climbing wall at school. I think you'll hold up.'

'And you love archaeology.' Alice zipped up her bag. 'You always said you wanted to go on an adventure.'

'Is it just us,' Arky asked his father, 'or is Lord Wright coming too?'

'He won't join us unless we find something,' replied Doc. 'But he's hired an expert in Asian artefacts, Professor Isobel Smythe. She's based in Mongolia and is making all the arrangements. We'll fly out to the nearest town in a few days' time, drive to the shepherd boy's yurt and look for more clues to the key. Of course, we don't want bad people to know what we are doing. Professor Smythe says we should pretend to be tourists. So, to make it look more real, we're taking a friend for you—Lord Wright's stepson. He'll join us the day we set out.'

'His stepson?' Arky hadn't heard of Lord Wright's stepson before. 'What's his name?'

'Poor thing.' Alice stiffled a giggle. 'Belvedere Elron Apollo Redford.'

'Belvedere Elron Apollo!' Arky snorted, wondering why rich people gave their kids weird names.

'Oh, don't call him that! He calls himself Bear.' Alice reached out and ruffled Arky's brown hair, giving Doc an anxious look.

'And you *will* be nice to Bear, for my sake,' said Doc, rather firmly. Arky was taken aback. His dad didn't normally ask him to be nice to someone. But, even if Bear was a snob, there was nothing he could do to ruin this trip.

Doc gave Alice a tense smile as he took the golden coin from Arky's hand.

Arky's heart leapt at the thought of the wild Mongolian mountains and the adventure that awaited him. But he wasn't sure he liked the worried look that had passed between his parents.

While Arky's father, Doctor Lukas Steele, made plans with his family to go to Mongolia, another man, sitting in a grand office full of artwork, was talking on the phone. His large shoulders strained against the fabric of an expensive suit.

'You've done well,' said Goran Rulec. 'One man, a woman and two children; they should be easy to watch. You'll find a welcome surprise in your bank account.'

Rulec put down the phone. His dark eyes flashed with malice as he walked from his office to his elevator. He pushed a button and was taken to a plush room in the basement. It was one of eight secret rooms in his mansion filled with ancient statues, intricate jewellery, marble carvings, mosaics, silks, furniture and artworks.

Rulec had inherited his wealth, and now owned many businesses. He soon discovered there were other wealthy people who wanted rare objects and didn't care how they got them. He controlled networks of grave robbers and thieves, and bought and sold rare and stolen artefacts. Even curators of museums were on his payroll. The spy in the house of his long-time enemy, Lord Wright, was his best work yet.

You're a smug toad, Wright, he thought. *You used to beat me at everything when we were at school together. You got invited to every party and you got the best girls. I'll enjoy taking this key from you.*

He smiled. His bright strong teeth contrasted with his wispy hair, which was brushed over a bald spot on his crown. His eyes, nearly always cold, flickered for a moment with genuine warmth.

'Ah, but to have some of Genghis Khan's treasure in my museum,' he said aloud. 'When his tomb is found, I'll be there first and the best things will be mine.'

The Expedition

Arky gritted his teeth against the bum-aching jolts and wished the day over as quickly as possible. He was riding in a rickety truck on a track that wound upwards between a ravine and a cliff. The road seemed to go forever.

The bumpy ride did nothing to improve the grumpy face on Bear, the dark-haired boy sitting beside him. Since they'd left the town, Bear's earphones had remained jammed in his ears, and his fingers drummed to the nonstop music coming from his computer.

Bear had arrived early that morning by car. He'd frowned in greeting at Arky and waited for his chauffeur to unload his bags. He didn't help Doc or Professor Smythe while they loaded the truck in preparation for their trip to the Mongolian high plains. He didn't even nod at Tue, the shepherd boy who'd found the gold coin, and who was travelling with them.

Suddenly, they hit a pothole. The truck lurched wildly. Arky gripped his armrest. As the window tilted towards the edge he could see a raging river at the bottom of the ravine. 'No one move!' he yelled.

The truck swayed dangerously. The wheels dug into the dirt, the engine roared, and small stones hurtled down the chasm. Arky's knuckles turned white. Bear's green eyes flashed fear for a second then he shut them, so Arky couldn't tell what he was thinking.

'How are you going, boys?' Doc called from the front seat. 'The track's getting very narrow and crumbly.'

'Good thanks, Doc,' Tue called back. He waggled his feet, showing off his new shoes. 'I don't worry.

Your lady driver is very good.' His large dark eyes oozed warmth and friendship.

'Professor Smythe *is* good,' Doc said.

'Isobel has lived here for a few years,' Arky told Bear. 'She speaks the language. She told us to call her Is.'

'I wish *you* spoke Mongolian and left me alone,' Bear said under his breath.

Slowly, with a gnashing of gears, the truck straightened and they bumped onwards.

'So, Bear,' Arky shouted, trying to engage Bear in conversation again, despite his rudeness. He sighed. His dad had asked him to be nice to Bear but it wasn't easy. The loud music coming from his laptop was really annoying. 'Think about how good it'll be camping out tonight.'

'Sleeping with sheep!' Bear finally removed his earphones.

'Goats,' corrected Tue, smiling.

Bear glared at Tue as if to say, *How horrible*.

Arky wondered *how horrible* Bear would be when his computer went flat. There would be no electricity, mobile phones or internet where they were going. And no rich stepfather to buy him gadgets.

Tue smiled again at Arky. His cheeks were red from the wind and his clothes were worn but he didn't even know the word 'complain'.

The truck hit another bump and stopped. There were shouts, so Arky stuck his head out the window. They were face to face with a dozen men leading heavily-loaded yaks. They began arguing with Is in Mongolian. 'They want her to back up,' translated Tue.

'Back up?' Arky blanched, eyeing off the edge of the dangerous ravine so close to their wheels. 'That'd be suicide! We could go over the edge.'

'Those men and yaks with their loads will not get past if she doesn't,' Tue said. 'Then we will be stuck forever. Someone has to move.'

Bear's face went red; he stood up, grabbed his laptop, clambered over a seat, ripped open the flap at the back of the truck and climbed out. He stood behind the truck, the music from his computer blaring. 'We're not backing up!' he yelled. 'My family's paying for this trip, so that's an order!'

Despite his protests, Is ground the gears and moved the truck closer to the edge of the ravine to let the yaks squeeze past on the inside. The animals waggled their ears nervously as the men urged them forwards.

'Get back in the truck,' Is shouted. 'Yaks can be cantankerous!'

Just as the first yak rounded the truck, Bear's music hit a high note. The yak, startled, kicked and bucked, shaking the truck. With the pressure of the other yaks behind it, it couldn't go backwards and escape the noise. So, snorting, head lowered and eyes rolling, it charged at the infuriating sound. It rammed Bear. His computer flew into the air, disappearing into the ravine.

The second yak bolted past the truck. It was knocked sideways by the first crazed beast and its hairy rump crashed into Bear. He lost his balance. For a heart-stopping second, Arky lost sight of Bear amongst the milling animals and the shouting men.

Then he appeared, gripping the second yak's tail, hanging over the ravine. His face was white as chalk, and his feet dangled in thin air.

The yak, grunting in terror, was slipping backwards on the crumbling edge.

Tue leapt from the truck. He grabbed one of the yak's horns and tried to haul it back onto the track. Arky scrambled down beside him, grabbing the beast's shaggy neck. Amidst the yelling and screaming, Arky and Tue pulled at the animal with all their might.

Within moments, one of the herders was beside them. Grunting and straining, they dragged the yak, and Bear with it, to safety.

It took Arky's dad a few seconds to get out of the front of the truck and around the yaks. He squatted beside Bear. 'You're safe, Bear,' he soothed, his eyes full of compassion. 'You can let go of the tail now.'

'No way, Doc.' Bear shook his head and gripped the yak's tail tighter. 'No way.'

'Yaks get nervous,' Doc warned. 'You don't want it bolting. So let go, please, and I'll help you to the truck.'

'Do what Doc says,' added Tue. 'Yaks are likely to poop if they're frightened.'

Bear's eyes widened. He looked up at the giant buttocks above his head. He let go and Doc hauled him to his feet. The yak snorted, its body stiffened and a massive brown stream splattered over Doc's and Bear's boots.

'Lucky!' Arky said, as the men driving the yaks laughed uproariously.

'Lucky!' Bear turned on Arky. 'Lucky! To be on this stupid stinking trip! I don't care if Genghis Khan and all his flipping treasure is hiding up the next valley, you can all stick it up your . . .'

Complaining yaks drowned out his words, as the herders goaded them into place so they could continue down the track.

Table Manners

The yurt appeared on the horizon just on dark. Tue's parents and his little sister ran alongside the truck, waving and laughing, until Is pulled up beside the goat pen. Tue's family helped them unpack. Tents, backpacks, stoves, fuel, ropes, gas bottles and food supplies were laid out on the ground.

Soon their tents were up and a fire was lit. Tue's mum came out of the yurt with a big pot of steaming meat. They sat around the fire and she served them dinner. Greasy meat floated on cracked plates. Arky found it very spicy.

Tue's family ate quickly. They slurped and ate with their mouths open and, amazingly, so did Is.

Then, in another surprise, Is rubbed her tummy and burped. It was a ripper! Arky was sure the flames on the campfire blew sideways.

Then Doc let fly with an even bigger one. Tue's father and mother nodded happily. Bear gawped in surprise.

'It's polite to burp after a meal in Mongolia,' Doc told them.

Arky quickly swallowed air and summoned up an explosion.

A wicked glint flashed across Bear's eyes and he began burping a song.

'It's one burp that's polite,' Is warned. But Bear couldn't be stopped.

Tue and his family stared in amazement as Bear's unusual tune went on for several more seconds. At least he was in a better mood.

After dinner, Tue's mother served warm yak milk for everyone. She handed a cup to Arky, who took a sip. It was thick, sticky and sour on his tongue. He glanced at Bear, who was sniffing it loudly. Arky didn't want to be bad-mannered, so he drank. It wasn't too bad in one go. He was met with a huge smile from Tue's mum. Bear pulled a face and gulped his milk down. Tue's mum gave him a hug. Bear was so shocked by the hug that his eyes bugged. Arky laughed.

❖

The boys' tent was pitched near the campfire. 'You'll sleep on a ground mat,' Doc said, as he unrolled two thin mats and put them in the tent.

'You could've brought mattresses!' Bear crossed his arms. 'You could have tried to make me comfortable.'

'I know you weren't here when we planned what we were taking.' Doc's voice was gentle. 'But we have one more day's drive. Then we'll set up a camp and we'll have to hike to where Tue found the gold coin. I don't think you'll want to carry a big mattress on a hike so you may as well toughen up now.'

Bear glared at Doc, turned and clambered into the tent.

Arky followed and climbed into his thick sleeping bag. He tried to get comfortable. Bear wriggled and grumbled under his breath, making it even harder for Arky to drift off.

'What a horrible place,' Bear muttered, for the tenth time.

'But think of the stories you'll tell when you get to school.' Arky tried to keep his cool.

'I'll be the new boy again,' Bear said. 'New boys keep their mouths shut.'

'Did you have friends at your last school?' asked Arky.

'Not really. I wasn't there long enough. I was expelled. Next year they're sending me to a boarding school in Switzerland . . .' He paused for a moment. 'Mother used to live in America till she married Lord Wright. He's my second stepfather and he doesn't like me.'

'Where's your mother now?'

'Linda's off doing a film. She's an actress.' Bear stared at the tent roof. Arky thought he sounded sad. 'That's why I'm here. A quest was a great way to get rid of me during school holidays. My stepfather made your dad take me on this trip. I know you don't want me here.'

'But you *are* here and I'm trying to like you. Why are you making it so hard?'

Bear gave a small laugh. 'Everyone pushes me around.'

'I guess I'd feel that way too if I were you.' Arky tried to imagine what it would be like living at boarding schools all the time.

There was silence for several minutes as Arky let the tension go out of the air. Then his stomach rumbled very loudly. 'Goat stew,' he groaned.

'Super greasy,' said Bear, and farted. 'That'll help keep the sleeping bag warm.'

'I could do with a nose peg!'

'Just don't light a match.'

BOOM!

An explosion outside the tent shook the air.

'That's one hell of a fart!' cried Bear, sitting bolt upright.

Doc was yelling. The boys tumbled from their sleeping bags and scrambled outside as bits of metal rained around them. Flames lit the night sky. The truck was on fire! The adults were running and dragging supplies away from the burning vehicle. Tue was gaping in shock from the doorway of his yurt, clutching his little sister to him.

Arky and Bear rushed to help. 'What happened?' shouted Arky.

'I don't know.' Doc groaned at the sight of so many ruined supplies.

'It's a write-off,' said Is, watching the burning hulk. 'The fuel tank's exploded!'

'How can a fuel tank just explode?' Arky was staring at the wreck in disbelief. It seemed impossible. 'How'll we travel tomorrow?'

'We can't,' said Doc. 'We won't be able to carry everything in our backpacks.'

Tue's family were shouting and waving their arms around.

'My parents are very angry about what has happened,' explained Tue. 'My father thinks now you will go home. My mother is sad I will have no job. Work is hard to get. My mother says men will come and try to get you to hire them to take you on your journey. She is sad because she cannot stop such things. My father says there is nothing anyone can do to stop bad folk. There are no police here, or law. Once, before the drought, people were honest. Now there are strangers in our land and people do things they shouldn't for money.'

'Like blow up our truck so they can take us?' asked Arky. 'Someone did it on purpose?'

'Sadly, Tue's family is right,' Is agreed. 'Don't be surprised if men arrive and offer to help us, for a small fee.'

'You'd better not hire them!' Arky was outraged. 'Not if they blew up our truck!'

'If no one turns up tomorrow, we can walk back and hire another vehicle,' said Is. 'It would be a long walk.'

'Down that horrible mountain?' Bear put his hands on his hips. '*You* can walk. Come back and get me later!'

'What does Tue's father think?' asked Doc. 'Would he let his son go out into the plains with people like that?'

Tue translated for his father. 'He will let me travel with men if they come by.'

'It's decided then,' said Doc. 'If men come, we'll continue with our quest.' He put his hand on Arky's shoulder, and said, 'It's a tough country, boys. Sometimes it's worth taking a few risks.'

'I'll ask Tue's dad if he wouldn't mind walking back to town and hiring us a new truck,' said Is. 'That way we will have a vehicle waiting for us when we return.'

'So, where are we going, anyway?' asked Arky.

'The Citadel of Skulls,' Is replied in a whisper.

'*Skulls?*' Bear's voice was full of disbelief. 'Like this place isn't horrible enough!'

'Why does it have such a scary name?' Arky ignored Bear's bad mood.

'Genghis Khan was a terrifying war lord, as you know,' Doc explained. 'His wild men would rage out of the mountains, surround a town, demand the surrender of the local king and take everything the people owned. But there was one proud king who refused to surrender to the Khan. He fought back. After many months, and lots of deaths on both sides, Genghis sent out a messenger to say he would let the king and everyone live if the king surrendered. The king agreed because his supplies were cut and everyone was hungry.

'But Genghis had no intention of keeping his promise. When the gates of the city were opened, Genghis and his army rode inside. Then he ordered everyone beheaded: men, women and children. When the massacre was over ninety thousand skulls were put in such large piles that they looked like the white towers of a city, glowing in the sunlight. *That* is the Citadel of Skulls.'

The Citadel of Skulls

'Men are coming!' Arky yelled, as the sun rose behind the camp.

Everyone was standing by the ruined truck. Tue's family eyed the two men who approached on horseback with yaks critically. The man on the leading horse jumped down and walked up to Doc. He smiled, but his eyes were lacking warmth. The other man, who had long hair dyed red, stayed on his horse.

'What happened to your truck?' said the first man.

'It blew up,' Doc replied.

'We were going to the Citadel of Skulls,' Is said. 'But sadly we can't now.'

'We learn that you should not give up when life gets difficult.' The man bowed low to Is. 'Perhaps we can help. My brother and I were going to town to pick up goods. My name is Yung.' He turned to his brother. 'What do you think, Fong? We would not want these people going home without seeing this beautiful land. We want tourists to visit, don't we? Then there will be more work for everyone.'

'We want you to feel welcome,' Fong replied. 'It is our duty to help you.'

'That's very kind.' Is smiled. She turned to Doc. 'What a wonderful offer! I'd love to go on, wouldn't you, boys?'

'Oh yes,' muttered Bear, sarcastically. 'Off to the Citadel of Skulls, with such nice men. *Very* kind!'

Tue's father approached the men and spoke intently. Is repeated what he was saying in a low whisper. 'Tue's father is now bargaining for the price we should pay them for each day they travel with us, so we are not cheated. He has settled for five dollars a day.'

Bear laughed. 'No one works for five dollars!'

'It is a lot of money up here,' Is said. 'Tue's family probably doesn't see that much in a month. That is why Tue's job is so important to them.'

Once the negotiations were finalised, Doc held out his hand to Yung. 'We're lucky you turned up,' he said. 'We'll enjoy travelling on horses.'

'Yes.' Is laughed. 'Travelling with horses and yaks will be quite an experience.' She patted Bear on the head, ruffling his hair.

Arky wasn't so sure the deal was a good one at all. He eyed their new companions apprehensively.

They had been riding for a few hours. Yung and Fong were leading the grumbling yaks across the plains and had fallen behind. The yaks couldn't carry everything, so they had packed only necessities: torches, tents, food, ropes, backpacks and wet weather gear.

Tue was walking beside Doc, leading his horse. 'These new shoes make me fly,' he said. 'Every step is like walking on a cloud.'

'I'm glad you like them.' Doc smiled. 'But you can ride, you know. You don't want to wear them out.'

'How many people were killed when Genghis Khan was in charge?' Bear asked, as they rode on. He'd finally stopped grumbling and had started taking in his surroundings.

He's a lot nicer without his computer, Arky thought.

'No one really knows,' replied Is from in front. 'We think that in all Genghis Khan's wars nearly forty million people died.'

'*Forty million?*' Bear raised his eyebrows. 'That's incredble.'

Is nodded. 'He was one of the most ruthless mass murderers of all time.'

'My family is descended from the Khan,' Tue said. 'Our people are proud of our history. Genghis was the greatest of all our ancestors. My grandmother told us we are the family from his 101st wife!

She says her grandmother was respected for having royal blood.'

'I can't imagine being proud of a tyrant,' Arky said.

'We're proud of our ancient kings,' Doc said. 'Most of them were tyrants too.'

'It's like a TV movie my mother would act in,' Bear said. 'She'd be the tragic queen, murdered in the Citadel of Skulls.'

'I'd love to watch TV,' replied Tue. 'We might have stories about our ancestors but to watch TV, that is magic! Is your mother really a star? I have seen magazines about stars.'

Bear nodded but didn't say anything more.

Late in the afternoon of the second day of hard riding, they arrived in a valley between snow-tipped mountains. This was where the Citadel of Skulls had been, and close to where Tue had found the gold coin. The men unloaded the animals and they camped beside the river that had once fed the ancient city.

Arky dismounted and rubbed his bum. 'It's a shame there's nothing much to see now,' he said, looking around.

'If you are lucky, you might find an arrowhead in the earth, left from the mighty battle,' Tue said. 'I have seen them.'

'Wow!' said Arky. 'I'd like that!'

As the sun disappeared behind the craggy mountains, Tue led the boys away from the camp. They began exploring in the shadows of the hills. Tue eagerly pointed out small white chips on the ground. 'Bones!' he said.

Arky bent down and dug up some earth. Within minutes he'd found a tooth and held it up. He was touching a tooth from a murdered person who lived almost a thousand years ago! It was sad, but exciting at the same time. He wanted to explore and find out more; one day he might become an archaeologist like his dad.

Soon he noticed ancient bricks and stones sticking out of the earth. Bear picked up an old cup handle. Tue found a rusty buckle. The boys continued hunting for artefacts until it became too dark to see and the smell of food called them back to camp.

As they sat around the fire, sparks flew into the night sky and a wind whistled eerily through the mountain valley. Nearby, Yung and Fong shifted uneasily and muttered between themselves. 'They're afraid of ghosts,' explained Tue. 'Not many people come here.'

'Weren't you scared when you came up here?' asked Bear. He seemed a little nervous himself.

'I was very hungry,' Tue said. 'There was grass here for the animals because of the river. Being scared is not as bad as being hungry. But I camped further away from this place just to be safe.'

'Are you scared now?' asked Arky, looking around at the darkness beyond the firelight.

'I am a bit,' Tue admitted.

'But you camped and herded goats on your own?' said Bear. 'And you didn't get lost?'

'I can visit my uncles and aunts out on the plain, or herd goats far, far away,' Tue said. 'I have been doing that since I was seven years old. Can't you go out on your own?'

'I can go to the shops on my own,' Arky said. 'But we don't go far from grown-ups in our country.'

'I'm never allowed out on my own in case someone kidnaps me,' Bear said. 'My parents are too rich.'

Arky and Tue both shook their heads. Arky wondered how people could be so poor in one country that children had to work as hard as adults, and yet in another country a child could be so rich that they had no freedom. 'It's a strange world,' he said, pleased he was just an ordinary kid.

'Are we far from where you found the gold coin?' he asked Tue.

'Deeper in the valley,' replied Tue. 'Where a little river falls out of the cliff. A slow day's walk.'

'The coin is very old,' Arky said, remembering how heavy it had felt in his hand. 'My dad thinks there may be more old things near where you found it. If we find them, then all the people in your valley will be better off.'

Tue shook his head, puzzled. 'I can't understand how. We have an old children's book. It is very old and my grandmother says it belonged to Genghis Khan, but it does not make us better off. *New* books are good. We all need new things.'

'Old things can be sold in our country for lots of money,' Arky explained. 'And if things are *really* old, and we find lots of them in one place, many tourists will come. Then they bring jobs and money with them.'

Tue looked amazed. 'It would be good to find these things for our people then!'

The horses nearby neighed restlessly. Yung stood up and walked towards them. Arky lowered his head and poked the fire. He hoped the wind had been loud enough to have covered their voices. After what his father had told him about artefact thieves, he wouldn't put it past these two men to try to rob them if they found anything valuable. Arky was glad Doc kept the gold coin safe in his hidden money belt. Even if the brothers were only looking for work, Arky didn't trust them.

Dead Swordsmen

It was drizzling when they set off again on their horses, leading a yak loaded with camping supplies and food. They had also packed torches and strong ropes to tether the animals. Doc told Yung and Fong to stay behind near the Citadel of Skulls. 'We want a few days to ourselves,' he explained. 'I'll pay you well to wait for us here.'

'We'll wait, boss!' Yung grinned. 'We'll enjoy a few days off, especially if we're paid for doing nothing.'

Arky didn't like his false smile. He was glad they were finally leaving the brothers behind.

Tue led them through a lightly wooded valley. Rabbits leapt out of their way and Bear pointed to shaggy goats clambering through the rocks. The drizzle soon turned to rain. But it definitely seemed that Bear had left his grumpiness behind.

A trickle of water ran down Arky's back. He shuddered with cold. Tue turned and smiled at him.

'It was raining when I found the big coin,' he said. 'We had no rain for years. I was happy even when the high mountains began to flood.'

Perhaps the rain was a lucky omen, Arky thought, although he'd prefer to be dry.

The animals slowed and stumbled on the steep, rocky path. Doc hobbled the horses and yak near a tree. 'We'll go on without the animals,' he said, 'and camp back here tonight.'

The rain had grown heavier and the mountains towered dark and wet above as the river roared angrily. Tue finally stopped them beside a large rock and pointed to a waterfall, falling from a cave high in the cliff above them. The stream crashed to a gravelly spot beside the river. 'This is where I found the coin.' He pointed. 'On the ground below that cave.'

All eyes went from the gravel, up the cliff to where the waterfall emerged. Not far from the mouth of the cave was a ruined goat track. Once it may have led up to the cave but over the years it had fallen away.

'What's that?' asked Bear, pointing to something under a ledge above the cave.

Doc reached into his backpack and pulled out his binoculars. He gasped and handed the glasses to Is. 'We've got to get up there!' she exclaimed, as she passed the glasses to Arky.

Slowly, Arky made out a mossy carving. 'You've got great eyesight, Bear! How did you see that?'

'*What* do you see?' asked Tue.

'A carved dragon head with a pearl in its mouth.' Is smiled, handing Tue the glasses. 'It's almost invisible under the moss and waterfall spray. But it's Genghis Khan's sign.'

'There's no way up,' said Doc. 'We'll have to go back to Tue's yurt and send out for climbing gear.'

'I can get up there.' Arky studied the path above. 'See the old goat track? If I took a rope I could get along it. Then, I think I could scale the last few metres to the cave and tie the rope to something so you could climb up.'

Is shook her head. 'It's too dangerous.'

'It's only a few metres,' argued Arky. 'I can crab sideways from the track. I can see hand- and footholds.'

'We'll come back first thing in the morning with a rope and look at it again,' Doc said. 'It's too wet and too late to make a decision.'

Arky couldn't wait till the morning to try again. When he finally made it to where the goat track had collapsed, the view was even more breathtaking than he'd imagined. He looked down, and realised it was higher than anything he'd climbed at school.

Doc was watching him from below with a grim face. 'Can you do it?' he called.

The cliff was slippery with moss but there were some good handholds. Arky looked up. There was a grip just in front of him. If he could hold it, it might support his weight till he could get onto the next foothold. He swallowed. 'Sure!' he called back, sounding more confident than he felt.

He reached out and clutched the rock. He stretched out his leg. The foothold held firm so he pulled his weight over to it. The long rope around his waist unbalanced him and he swayed. He waited till he recovered.

Slowly, he crabbed out along the cliff until the waterfall spray made it really slippery and the space between the rocky outcrops he was using grew further apart.

There was a small shelf not far from the cave, but he could only get to it if he jumped. He was sure he could make it, but if he didn't, it would be a horrible fall to the ground below. It was a terrible risk. He looked behind him. He didn't fancy going back and the cave was *so* close.

He took a risk, sprang and landed safely on the shelf.

Several frightened heartbeats later, he regained his self-control. All he had to do now was to get to one last rock, then he could reach up and grasp the ledge to the cave. The rock was just a bit further than a step away. It was small and slick with moss and water droplets.

Arky forced himself not to look down and, extending his leg full-length and pressing his body against the cliff, he stretched out. His foot touched the rock, but then he overbalanced. He managed to run his hands across the moss, pulling himself up and across so he stood precariously below the cave.

The sound of the waterfall almost drowned his thoughts as he cautiously reached up to the ledge below the cave. All of a sudden, his right foot slipped. One hand gripped the ledge but the other hadn't found a hold. With his heart hammering, he slammed his free hand into the cliff, grabbing at the thick moss. It held him for a second and, before the moss gave way, he got his right foot back onto the rock, sprang slightly and hauled himself up to the cave ledge.

He'd made it! He waited for the sweat to cool on his brow and his heart to settle. Below him his father's face was deathly white. Is had her hands across her eyes and Bear was open-mouthed. 'I thought you were a goner!' Bear shouted.

'Archibald Steele!' Is yelled, seeing Arky safe. 'You're an idiot!'

Arky turned, looking for a place to tie the rope. The cave was narrow and dark but there was a boulder lying across some other stones, just beside the stream that led to the waterfall. It took him a few minutes to secure his rope and lower it down.

Doc was first to clamber into the cave. 'I'll never let you do anything like that again,' he said, hugging Arky.

Tue shinnied up the rope in seconds. Bear took several goes to work out how to climb. Is showed him how to grip the rope and use his legs on the rocks to pull himself up. When he finally got to the cave he was shaking and his lips were white.

Is arrived in the cave just as it began to rain heavily outside. 'We're dry in here at least,' she said, shaking droplets from her coat.

'But the rain will have to run somewhere,' Tue warned. 'This stream might get bigger.'

'We'll make it quick then,' Doc said, taking torches from his backpack.

'Very quick.' Bear nervously drummed his fingers on his thigh.

❖

Arky led the way into the cave, which extended into a tunnel. The torches lit the cavern and made the water seeping down the walls glisten. The explorers stumbled several times on the cold, slimy rocks. They hadn't gone far when Arky saw an odd shape lying on the ground.

'It looks like an old breastplate,' Doc said, picking up the rusty metal. 'It's hard to tell how long it's been here, but it's a wonderful find.' The excitement in his voice helped everyone move forward faster.

The stream beside them became deeper and forced them up onto a ledge etched into the wall. It was free of stones so walking became easier. 'You can tell this creek has flowed very strongly over the years,' said Doc.

'It's lucky this ledge is here,' Bear said. 'I don't like walking in the water. It's freezing.'

They moved further into the mountain until they came to a small cascade. They climbed up the ledge and stopped at the top, where there was a wide cavern.

Bear gasped as Arky's torch lit up a pile of skulls almost in front of him. The hollow eye sockets glared at the intruders. Is gave a stifled scream. A skeleton, its own head resting in its lap, sat beside the skulls, guarding the way forward. Its arms hung at its side. Its gleaming skull shone in the torchlight. Its teeth formed a gruesome smile.

The Raging Torrent

'Eureka!' cried Doc, as their torches lit battleaxes and spears resting on more headless skeletons. There were piles of them on the worn ledges of the cavern. Over the bones, a film of slime shimmered like glass. 'There must be around fifty men. We're onto something now!'

Arky shut his eyes for a second, not believing what he was seeing—or hearing. The water from the stream bubbled and gurgled, like men taking their last breath. The hairs rose on the back of his neck. Tue squealed and muttered something about ghosts. Arky thought it best to open his eyes again.

Bear edged around the sitting skeleton towards a pile of rusting armour. He bent and lifted a glimmering knife, bejewelled with red stones. 'How old is this lot?' he asked.

Doc was counting the skulls. 'The armour looks right for the Khan era,' he replied.

'Who are these people?' asked Arky.

'These bodies could be Genghis Khan's missing soldiers.' Is breathed out slowly, amazed they had made such a find.

'It's possible,' replied Doc. 'So, please boys, don't touch anything. I want you to go carefully. The key might be in here so I don't want you messing anything up.'

Bear carefully put the knife back where he'd found it. He returned to stand beside Arky as Doc and Is moved into the cavern to explore.

Tue, ashen-faced, turned and walked away from the skeletons. 'I have to go back to the entrance where there is light,' he called as he left the cavern. 'I can't stay with ghosts. Being here is bad luck. Bad things will happen. I feel it in my bones.'

'Bones,' sniggered Bear. 'I feel the bones had the bad luck!'

Arky snorted with laughter. As his laugh echoed eerily, he wondered if his laughter came from fear. The skulls stared hauntingly at him. What sort of monster had killed these men and placed their skulls so precisely in a pyramid?

'It's creepy to think someone piled up all those heads,' Bear said, mirroring his thoughts. 'Then someone sat that guy on a rock with *his* head in his lap.'

'That must be the Keeper of Secrets!' Arky remembered the old manuscript his dad had found. 'The one who hid the key. He said he'd be the first to smile at the key hunter! No wonder Dad's so excited.'

'I thought the Keeper of Secrets was looking at me as I came in,' Bear said, 'but all the skulls in the pile are looking in the same direction.' He moved closer to the skulls, his torch highlighting the dark eye sockets.

'Could they be looking *past* you?' Arky said thoughtfully. 'Like, looking at something in their past? The last thing they did was to help hide a great treasure. Their ghosts are keeping the secret.' The puzzle before him made him put aside his fear and he moved to stand beside Bear.

'And perhaps that's why they were arranged the way they are,' Bear said. 'To give us a clue to help us find the key.'

'So, they are looking past us,' Arky said. 'What's behind us?'

Bear and Arky turned their torches across the cavern and over the creek, following the gaze of the skull's empty eye sockets. In the opposite rock wall, faded with age and almost hidden by the slick algae, was a carving. Bear and Arky rock-hopped across the stream and studied the work closely. All they could make out were three interlocking circles.

'It's not very helpful,' Arky said. 'But it must be important or someone wouldn't have spent time chipping these odd shapes into the rock. The old manuscript said the coin was part of a three-part key.'

'It doesn't *look* like a key,' Bear said.

'If the coin fits into the first hole here,' Arky said, pointing to the first circle, 'then it might lock the other two circles together.'

'The coin is flat,' he added. 'Maybe we should look for something circular that's about the same thickness.'

'There's no black sludge underneath the carving,' Bear said. 'So water hasn't reached this high. The gold coin must have been low down and carried away by a flood.'

'And that's how Tue found it.' Arky smiled. 'It was washed out of this tunnel. But how did it get—' As he spoke there was a disturbing rumbling sound. 'What's that?' He looked around to see what it could be. His dad and Is were high in the cavern on the other side. Their torchlight wavered as they searched.

'It doesn't sound good.' Bear was also listening intently to the distant noise. 'We should get back to the other side.'

Arky realised the creek was rising! The rocks they had hopped across had disappeared. 'Hurry!' he cried.

Bear and Arky began wading back. The little stream had become fierce, and it pulled at their legs. Arky slipped. Bear grabbed him by the belt, trying to stop him from being carried away. He struggled to pull him to safety but Arky's weight was too much on the slippery rocks. Bear fell on top of Arky and they both went under. Their torches flew from their hands and were carried away by the strengthening force of the water.

Both boys were tumbled over and over and hurled down the cascade, which had now become a torrent. Arky's breath was knocked out of him. By the time he pushed his head above water he was gasping in terror and Bear was still clinging to his belt. The cold sapped his strength and he struggled under Bear's weight. As the water rolled him under again, Arky wondered vaguely why Bear didn't let go and fend for himself.

Arky struggled for the two of them. Suddenly, his feet ground against some pebbles. He rammed his toes down, almost managing to clamber to his feet, but Bear's weight dragged him over.

'Let go!' Arky screamed, but his cry was drowned out by the raging water.

It slammed him into a rock, crushing the breath from his lungs. In the dark, he grabbed the hard stone surface, digging in with his nails. The slime, and Bear's weight, made it impossible to hang on. Gasping for breath, the water ripped him away from his hold. He struggled to keep his head up as he was hurtled through the cavern.

His heart sank as a glimmering light in the distance told him that in seconds the waterfall would plunge them over the cliff.

Meanwhile, Tue had made his way back to the cave entrance. He knew light kept ghosts away. *No one ever sees ghosts in daylight*, he told himself over and over. But he couldn't shake the terrible fear that something bad could happen.

He felt the torrent coming before he heard it. He had been raised in the wilds and his sense of self-preservation was good. Almost without thinking, he grabbed the free end of the climbing rope that was lying on the cavern floor. He scrambled with it up to a ledge inside the cave. Quickly he looped the rope around his waist. He braced his feet against two other rocks so he could resist any water pressure.

If the water takes me from here, he thought, *the rope will help me. I will fall, but I won't hit the ground. The other end is secured to the boulder Arky tied it to so we could climb up.*

Within seconds of securing his line he saw torches fly past. Their lights flashed around the tunnel before they were shot down the waterfall. Then, to his horror, he saw the heads of his friends being swept towards oblivion.

❖

Arky's heart hammered in his chest. He thrashed out again and again, trying to make the rock ledge he knew must be nearby. Then, as the mouth of the cave shone light into his eyes, he saw something.

It was a line, just in front of him. It ran up from the water and across the tunnel. He pulled both his arms up and lunged through the water. His fingers just touched the rope. He gripped and it held him. Bear seemed to realise Arky had somehow stopped their descent and grabbed him more tightly. Arky hoped his belt wouldn't break, or his trousers come off.

Bear's weight was almost too much. But the fear of death was worse. Using a strength he never knew he had, Arky pulled himself along the rope to the ledge above the waterline. He soon saw what was keeping him alive.

Tue was lying flat on the ledge. The rope around his waist was digging savagely into his hips. His legs strained against a rock and his face was contorted with pain. He was using every bit of his energy to brace the weight of Arky and Bear against the raging waters. If his legs buckled or he moved, he would be pulled from the ledge and they would all be doomed.

Although Arky was beside the ledge he couldn't get onto it. He couldn't swing his legs up because Bear was pulling him down. He couldn't let go of the rope, even with one hand, because he wasn't strong enough to keep his hold with the other. He was stuck hanging centimetres from safety.

Bear pulled himself onto Arky's shoulders and, using him as a ladder, clambered onto the ledge beside Tue. Then he grabbed Arky and hauled him onto the ledge.

Arky lay on the rock shelf gasping with exhaustion. Bear seemed to wipe away tears running down his face.

When the exhaustion left Arky, he moved beside Tue and patted his shoulder in thanks. Tue removed the rope from his reddened and bruised hips. The three boys linked arms and closed their eyes. Arky had never felt so tired. He was so weary he'd even stopped feeling cold. A dreamy sleep overwhelmed him and he was glad.

'You can't sleep!' screamed Tue, so loudly that Arky's ears hurt. 'Wake up! Wake *up*!'

'Stop hitting Arky!' Bear cried. But Tue ignored him, viciously pinching Arky's cheek.

Arky opened his eyes. 'Ouch!' he cried. 'Why'd you do that?'

'You are cold and the water is sucking out your life,' Tue said. 'Stand up and jump up and down!'

'Hypothermia!' Bear tore Arky's wet jacket off and began shedding his own clothes.

Through the fog in Arky's brain, he realised Tue was right and he forced himself to move.

'Your dad's coming!' Tue pointed to torchlights shining on the ledge from the darkness behind them.

As he spoke, the climbing rope whipped off the ledge beside Tue and vanished into the swirling waters.

Secrets Revealed

Is and Doc took off Arky's and Bear's tops and jackets and wrapped the boys in dry clothes. Sunlight beamed in from outside. The rain clouds lifted and the torrent became a little stream again. The world became quieter.

'We're going back now,' Doc said. 'It's far too dangerous here. Are you ready to climb down the rope?'

Arky nodded, feeling the warmth flood back into his arms and legs. 'I'll be okay in a minute,' he said.

'It won't help,' Is cried, pointing. 'Look! The rock with the rope around it has gone!'

Tue stared at the place where the rope and rock had last been seen. 'It's been washed over the cliff!' He paled, realising that if he had not undone the rope around his waist after Arky and Bear were saved, he'd have been dragged away with it—over the waterfall to his death. 'We are very lucky! We are all alive. This is a good omen. The gods are with us.'

'But what now?' Bear was horrified at the thought of trying to climb down the cliff without a rope.

'If I could get down the way I got up I could go for help,' Arky suggested, as he edged to the mouth of the cave and surveyed the steep cliff into the valley. The few handholds he'd used to get up to the cave had been washed away. His heart sank.

'There's no way,' Doc said. 'The way back is gone!'

A stunned silence weighed them all down for several minutes while they thought about their problem.

'We should try to travel through the mountain,' Doc finally suggested. 'There was a lot of water in that flood. There must be an entrance somewhere higher up, where the water flows in.'

'Back into the dark!' Bear groaned, shivering at the thought.

'You boys need to eat.' Is lifted her backpack from her shoulders and handed the boys their lunches. 'You'll need your strength if we are to try this.'

The boys gobbled their sandwiches, until Arky noticed his dad and Is weren't eating.

'We'll keep our food for later,' Doc said, noticing Arky's glance. 'We don't need to eat just now.'

'But I'd like to hear something that would cheer me up,' Is muttered.

'This might . . .' Arky tried to look more confident than he felt. 'We think we found something really interesting.'

Doc's eyes widened as Arky and Bear told him of the circle carving they'd discovered before the flood carried them away.

'We have to go back to the headless skeleton,' Doc said. 'He might hold other secrets.'

Under the light of a torch, Doc noticed the skeleton's

skull was supported on its bony lap by a bronze plate. He lifted the skull carefully.

To Arky's delight the plate had a hole in it. 'The hole looks about the same size as the coin,' he said.

Doc held the plate close to the torch. He turned it over. Deep lines were engraved on both sides.

'See if the coin fits,' urged Arky.

Doc undid his hidden money belt and pulled out the coin.

Bear pushed it into the old bronze plate. It fitted!

Doc shone the torch over the skeleton again. 'One hand's missing.'

'That was the hand closest to the river,' Is said. 'I suspect it held the gold coin and, finally, after many years it fell off, and lay by the water until it was taken in a flood.'

'Look at the other hand,' Tue said. 'Is there anything in it?'

Doc shone the torch onto the other skeletal hand. The fingers were looped with old leather.

'Are they reins?' Tue asked.

'They could be, but they've rotted too badly to

tell.' Doc moved the torch over the leather. 'Why do you ask?'

'In the old book at home I told you about is a riddle,' Tue replied. '*What does death hold?* And there is a picture of the death god sitting on a throne and a dark horse beside him. The god holds a coin in one hand, the reins to his horse in the other, and a skull is on his lap.'

'What's the answer?' everyone asked.

'The end of riches, the end of thoughts and the ride to enlightenment.'

'I have to see that book when we get back,' said Is. 'Especially if it really is as old as you say.'

Doc lifted the bony fingers of the other hand, which was resting on the ground. He scraped away years of dirt and grime. Suddenly, there was a glint of metal.

'It's the third part of the key!' cried Arky.

It was the size of a dinner plate with a thick rim, etched with deep lines and it had a hole in it. Taking the coin and the bronze plate from the skeleton's lap, Doc snapped the three pieces together. He held it up.

'It's a big round key,' Bear said.

'What sort of door has a keyhole big enough for that to fit inside?' asked Arky.

'We should move on now.' Is looked ahead into the darkness. 'We have what we came for, and we don't want our torches to fail.'

Everyone nodded reluctantly, so Doc placed the three parts of the key carefully into his backpack. Is held the torch and led the way, followed by the boys, with Doc coming last, to make sure everyone kept together. The stream burbled and tumbled beside them and the cavern's roof became lower. Is and Doc had to bend almost double. It was decided that Arky should go first, as he was the shortest and could walk upright, holding the torch.

Not only did the tunnel become smaller, it also became steeper and more slippery. The first torch ran out after a few hours. The second torch led them to a place where the creek flowed through a low cavity and they had to crawl if they wished to continue their journey.

Arky's knees and elbows hurt as they bumped on rocks. In places water sloshed into his mouth, so he breathed through his nose. The noise of the rushing water filled his ears. His clothes dragged and rubbed, and made the going hard and slow. The water chilled him again, and he wished he were back in his home in a hot bath.

Luckily, the torch provided enough light to see ahead and the tunnel didn't get any smaller but eventually opened out and everyone stood, exhausted and wet. Fresh air fanned Arky's face and despite the dark, he realised they must be close to escaping the tunnel.

'We can't stop for a rest,' Doc said. 'We have to move as fast as possible.'

'Walk fast, with groin chafe! My lucky day!' Bear pulled at his wet clothes in frustration.

He walked with his legs wide apart, groaning every so often and scratching at his crotch until his body heat finally dried his clothes. Eventually starlight and a thin moon showed them they were free of the mountain and that they had arrived beside a sheltered ledge.

'I think we should stop and rest.' Is sounded as exhausted as Arky felt. 'It's too dark to try to get down the mountain. Perhaps we should share out what remains of our food and sleep for an hour or two. That should get our strength back.'

No one argued and, despite Arky's belief that he could never fall asleep on rocks, he lay down and knew nothing more until he was shaken awake.

The following day, they descended a ridge and by late afternoon found themselves back by the stream, not far from their camp. Arky was so hungry! He couldn't wait to get back to their tents and the hobbled animals.

As they came closer to their campsite, Arky began to look around for the yak or the horses. He wondered if they might have shaken their ropes loose and run off. 'Shouldn't we see our tents or the horses by now?' he asked.

'Are we in the right valley?' Bear looked around, bewildered.

'We are,' replied Tue, stooping and holding up food wrappers that had been thrown against a tree. 'Someone has stolen our things!'

'Our tents and everything!' Bear shouted, in disbelief. 'And my money!'

'I didn't think Yung and Fong would do that to us,' said Doc, upset, 'especially as they promised to look after us.'

'How much money were you carrying, Bear?' Is asked.

'A couple of hundred,' Bear replied. 'But I've still got my credit card.'

'A couple of hundred dollars is a fortune up here,' Is explained. 'I realise it isn't much for you, but you should have told us you were carrying it. Leaving money like that lying around was foolish.'

Bear glared at her.

'The brothers must have followed us and seen we were stuck in the cave,' Tue said. 'They would have been glad, because they could get more from us dead than alive!'

'So now what?' Bear was back to his old angry self. 'I'm to blame for getting us robbed! How come I'm blamed? As if it's not bad enough! I'm starving and cold and fed up and—'

'And don't go there!' cried Arky. 'Don't start complaining. It won't help us at all.'

'And it better not rain!' Bear shouted. 'And I will complain! I didn't want to be here and now I'm screwed!'

Tue's eyebrows lowered and his eyes darkened. He looked Bear up and down. Without a word, he turned and took off into the rocks, vanishing before anyone could stop him.

'Now look what you've done!' Arky yelled at Bear.

'Stop that!' Doc stepped towards them. 'Fighting's not helping us. If it's anyone's fault, it is mine. I should have made us go back when the truck blew up. I shouldn't have risked travelling with those men. I was so eager to hunt for the key, I didn't think of a situation like this.'

'Let's not think about what's gone wrong,' Is interrupted. 'Look, it's not raining. There are trees around and I have some matches in my backpack. We should gather wood and make a fire. We'll sleep here tonight and then we'll hike back to Tue's yurt.'

'Hike on an empty stomach!' Bear looked more miserable than Arky felt.

'Will Tue come back?' Arky asked.

'He's not used to Westerners,' Is said. 'People in Mongolia dislike rude people. They feel being impolite is an offence to their mountain gods. He may have gone off for a while to calm down. When he comes back you will both owe him a big apology!'

When the flood had washed the climbing rope away, Yung's binoculars were focused on the cave high up the cliff. Through the glasses he could see their worried faces as they realised they were trapped. He smiled. 'They will die up there. There is no way down,' he'd said to Fong, who was sitting beside him. 'We will come back in a few weeks when they are dead. We will climb up and get what they came for.' He chuckled. 'Rulec will reward us.'

'We should take everything they own so no one can find them,' Fong replied. 'We can sell their things in town while we wait for the search for them to die down.'

'Good idea,' agreed Yung.

As the thieves headed towards town the following day, Yung had a second thought. There may have been another way out of the cave. 'What if we made a mistake by leaving too soon?'

Fong pulled up his horse. 'If they return with the treasure and we lose it, Rulec will have us killed. He does not tolerate mistakes.'

Yung scratched his head and thought over the situation. 'You go on to town. When the word goes out they are missing, people will hunt for two men with horses and yaks. Sell the horses and yaks and wait for me at our gang's headquarters. I will lie low and watch Tue's yurt for a few more days. I will join you in town when all is well.'

An Ancient Book

It became dark early and the travellers huddled around the bright fire they had managed to make. Small sparks flew into the air and Arky's stomach growled loudly. Bear's guts gurgled and Doc's tummy rumbled like an earthquake. A weird squeak erupted from Is's belly. 'Symphony of the starving,' Is quipped.

'We're all hungry,' Doc said. 'But people can survive ten days without food as long as they have water.'

'We'll have a long walk back,' Is warned. 'You boys will have to be tough.'

'I've got a bit of fat on me,' Bear said bravely. 'I can probably do without a bit of food. But I feel rotten. It's my fault Tue's gone. I should apologise.'

Arky was surprised by Bear's words. He didn't think Bear apologised very often.

'Hungry?' said a voice from the darkness.

Everyone spun around. Tue walked into the firelight carrying two squirrel-like animals. He threw them onto the flames and rubbed his hands near the heat. 'When I was up here last, I made some snares and hid them, in case I came back some day. So I went to get them, set them up and waited.' He smiled happily. 'Now we burn off their fur and put them in the coals till they are hot.'

'Marmots,' Doc said as he poked the furry little creatures with a stick.

Later, the smell of roasting marmot made Arky's mouth water. Bear stood up and put his arm around Tue. 'I've never been good at having friends,' he said. 'Thank you, Tue, for feeding us.'

'Thank you, Tue!' everyone chimed in.

When Tue deemed the marmots cooked, he pulled off their heads and ripped out their guts with his bare hands. Then he tore the marmots into pieces and handed the meat out.

'It tastes a bit like how cat pee smells,' Bear grumbled, as he bit into his food. Then seeing Tue's surprise, he added, 'But I'm sure they taste better as you go on.'

'Can you catch more on our way back?' asked Doc.

'Of course. But, there is no wood on the plains. We burn their fur off with grass and eat them raw out there.'

Bear and Arky stared in dismay at the thought of the next night's menu.

'Did you know it is believed Mongolian marmots caused the bubonic plague that spread through Europe and killed millions of people in Genghis Khan's time?' Doc said, as Arky was about to bite into his dinner.

'I'd rather you hadn't told me that.' Is stared gloomily at her portion.

Arky tried not to choke as he swallowed. As the smelly grease ran down his fingers, he wondered how hungry he would have to be to eat raw marmot.

A few days later, Tue's mother ran to meet the exhausted travellers as they made their way towards the yurt. She took one look at their drawn faces and their bedraggled clothes and grabbed Tue to her. Arky turned to look back across the plains. The setting sun made the rocks glimmer and the grass turn grey. He couldn't believe they had made it back safely!

Once inside the yurt, the boys collapsed on the goatskin rugs. Tue's mother stoked the fire with dried yak dung and a goat stew was soon simmering in the pot.

Arky's mouth watered when Tue's little sister finally spooned the meat into their bowls.

He fell upon his food like a wolf, bolting it down. He licked his plate when he finished and burped loudly, but then wished he hadn't, because all the food erupted in the back of his throat. His eyes watered and Tue's sister laughed.

'Better than raw marmots,' Is said, sipping her stew carefully.

Arky didn't want to remember the marmots at all. He was sure the revolting animals had upset his guts because he had been farting all the way back. It was fine to let one go while walking but now, inside the yurt, he could feel his lower gut start to bubble and fizz.

As everyone sat around the smoky fire, and just as Tue showed his parents the ancient key they'd found in the cave, a terrible smell filled the yurt.

Tue's mother waved her hand in front of her face as she picked up the key. As Is was explaining the importance of their find, Bear let go with a resounding, cheek-clanging burst of gas. The pong was so awful that Doc leapt to his feet and opened the yurt door to let the cold air flow inside.

'Say "excuse me"!' Is ordered the boys. 'One more of those from either of you and you'll sleep outside tonight!'

When everyone could breathe again, Tue's sister got out the old children's book. Arky held his hands out for it. It wasn't very big, but it was heavy. 'It's made of vellum,' Doc explained, as he peered over Arky's shoulder. 'Vellum is calfskin. It's what people wrote on back then.'

Doc touched the pages and looked at the artwork. 'It has Genghis's symbol on the cover,' he said, opening the book.

Tue smiled proudly. 'All Genghis Khan's grandchildren got this book on his fifty-fourth birthday, the one before he died. That's what my grandmother said.'

'So, once there were probably hundreds of copies,' said Arky.

'Over the centuries they would have worn out and been thrown away,' Doc said. 'It's amazing this copy has lasted and is in such good condition.'

'My grandmother's family treasured it,' said Tue. 'My father treasures it.'

Bear moved to sit beside Arky. 'Look at the

borders,' he said. 'Every page has dozens of tiny perfect golden dragons painted around it.'

'There are 999 dragons in the book,' Tue said. 'We counted them.'

'That's the Chinese number for enlightenment,' Doc said. 'And nine is considered a very lucky number, it was also the number for the Emperor of China, and for the Khan!'

'Can you read it?' Bear asked.

Tue shook his head. 'No one writes like that now, so we can't read it all properly. My parents tell us some things that were told to them. It's full of riddles and mysteries.'

'It must have taken forever to make.' Arky brushed his hand over an intricate design.

'It's *gruesome*,' Bear said, peering over Arky's other shoulder. 'It's full of skulls and skeletons.'

'Not every page,' Arky said, turning a page, 'here is a lovely temple with gongs drawn around it.'

Everyone crowded around. 'This is the temple at Ulaangom,' Is said, immediately. 'I did some study up there a while ago. It is known for its old gongs, which the monks still ring. The monks were murdered after Genghis's death, and it was abandoned for centuries. Now, some very poor monks live there.'

'What does it say underneath the picture of the monastery?' Arky asked.

'What walks in silence and cannot be seen?' read Is, who was an expert in ancient Mongolian. 'What is always expected but never welcome?'

'So what's the answer?' Arky looked at everyone. 'What walks in silence and can't be seen, and is expected but not welcome?'

'One of your farts,' said Tue, scowling.

'Turn the page, Arky,' Doc said, ignoring Tue's complaint.

Arky turned the page. 'It's a skeleton.'

'Death!' answered Bear. 'It's an old riddle. Death is always expected but not welcome.'

'Not quite,' said Is. 'Look at the skeleton. It has no hands. The real answer is the Hand of Death!'

'The legendary Hand of Death is supposedly in the tomb of Genghis Khan,' breathed Doc, awed by the answer.

'And what is the Hand of Death, exactly?' asked Arky.

'It was a hand forged in gold.' Doc began another explanation. 'It had a pin underneath it that made the hand spin and one finger pointed outwards. The hand was supposed to have been kept in an armoured glove. If Genghis thought there was a traitor in his group, the hand was spun. Whoever it pointed at was the traitor. That man was then killed, in a gruesome way. The hand was supposed to be magic and always right.'

'Was it magic?' Arky wondered how the golden hand worked. He wasn't sure he believed in magic.

'No,' Is said. 'If he thought there was a traitor amongst his close friends, he told a few people that he planned to take out the hand and expose the traitor. Then Genghis would wait and see who was the first person to try to leave before he spun the

Hand of Death. The guilty man gave himself away through fear of the so-called magic.'

'Genghis didn't believe in magic,' Doc said, 'but he knew other people were very superstitious and he played mind games with them.'

'And you said he's supposedly hidden the hand in his tomb,' Arky said slowly, thinking. 'And this old book is the Book of Clues! Just like the Keeper of Secrets said—it's hidden well, yet easy to find!'

'And no one back then wondered why Genghis Khan gave them to all his grandchildren!' Doc laughed. 'Now I understand why he didn't have much faith in his family. They don't sound too bright. And his sons obviously never read books to their kids!'

'It must be the next clue to help us find his treasure!'

'Could Genghis's tomb be under the monastery?' Arky asked. 'Or maybe you get to it through the temple? Perhaps there is a secret tunnel?'

Doc nodded. 'Maybe those monks died so the tomb could be built.'

As he spoke, the goats outside the tent began bleating wildly. 'There's someone out there,' Tue said.

Tue and Arky rushed to the open door and looked out. Arky thought he saw a shadow dart between some rocks. He pointed.

'It could have been a wild dog,' said Tue.

But Arky was worried. Someone could have been listening to them through the open yurt door.

Trouble

The following day the team set out for Ulaangom. They arrived after a long and bumpy ride, which had included several stops for Arky and Bear to unload what was left of the marmots.

The town's buildings were nestled under towering mountains. A raging river flowed from a gleaming glacier and, in the distance, a waterfall sent spray high into the air, making a spectacular rainbow.

As they drove down the main street they dodged carts, yaks and families leading funny two-humped camels. Speeding motorbikes and ancient taxis dashed around them. Shops and street stalls crowded the edge of the road. Most of the buildings were old and worn. Everyone stared at the strangers as they pulled up beside an old hotel.

'This is the coldest place on earth in winter,' Doc told the boys, as they piled out of the truck.

Once they were in their room, Bear went straight to the TV and turned it on. 'I hope they've got internet,' he said. Tue glued his eyes to the TV.

'Well, Tue won't move for hours.' Is smiled.

'Is and I have to go and talk to some officials,' Doc said. 'The government wouldn't take too kindly to us wandering into old temples without permission. We don't want you getting into trouble while we are out, so we can hire someone from the hotel to look after you.'

'We can be trusted.' Bear smiled, turning on the charm. 'We're safe in the hotel. And Tue would laugh if we had a babysitter. He's been allowed out on his own for years.'

'You promise you won't go anywhere?' Doc looked stern. 'We know artefact thieves are around.

I have to trust you'll stay in your room while we are busy.'

Arky nodded. 'We don't need minding for just a couple of hours. Not with three of us here.'

Shortly after Is and Doc left, Bear started pacing the room. 'I'm bored,' he said, going to the window and looking out. 'There's a stall opposite, selling chips and things. What if I just nick out and buy stuff?'

'We shouldn't.' Arky joined Bear by the window. He was bored too. He couldn't understand anything on the television and there was nothing to do in the room. 'It *is* only a few metres away,' he said. 'It's not really going anywhere, is it? And Tue can help us talk to the shopkeeper.'

'Come on, Tue,' Bear called, turning to the door. 'We'll only be a second.'

Tue didn't move, so Bear went over and turned the TV off. 'Come on!'

The street was more crowded than Arky had realised. Several people jostled him and, before he knew it, he was separated from Bear and Tue. By the time he got to the shop there was no sign of his friends. *They must have gone down there*, he thought, walking towards a narrow road filled with small stalls.

He hadn't gone far when a hand was clamped firmly over his mouth and he was dragged into a darkened alley. Terrified, Arky struggled as he was manhandled through run-down streets. Despite the man's vice-like hold, Arky twisted and fought. Seeing he was being dragged further and further away from the hotel, he desperately bit down hard on the hand of the brute holding his mouth.

The man yelped and let go. Arky ran for his life. He tore blindly round a corner and crashed headlong into someone. He was knocked to the ground. 'Help!' he yelled, hoping the person would come to his aid.

'My travelling friend,' said a voice. 'How fortunate to meet like this!'

Arky looked up. Yung was standing over him, his eyes full of malice. Arky stumbled to his feet and accidently headbutted Yung in the groin. Yung doubled over, gripping his privates.

Arky, his head spinning, made another dash for freedom, but the man with the bitten hand had caught up with him. He grabbed Arky's jacket, swung him around and pushed him against a wall.

Yung, his eyes watering, moved awkwardly over to Arky and pinioned his arm behind his shoulder. 'You'll pay for that,' he groaned.

'*You'll* pay,' cried Arky, fighting the painful hold. 'Police! Police!'

'Shout all you like,' Yung said. 'The police won't come. This isn't a place they visit unless they are invited.' Clutching Arky firmly, they frog-marched him through the shabby streets.

Arky struggled and yelled, hoping his desperate cries would bring someone to his aid, but the people walking nearby either turned their faces to a wall or stopped abruptly and walked the other away. Arky realised they were frightened of Yung and the man who held him. No one was going to help him and he should save his strength. He stopped struggling, but his heart was hammering in his chest. He tried to think through his panic. If only he had obeyed his father then this wouldn't be happening. Why was Yung kidnapping him and what was behind it? Maybe someone wanted money.

'Did someone pay you to kidnap me?' he blurted.

'I don't know what you are talking about.' Yung pulled Arky into a dilapidated house.

'My father is poor,' he explained, as one of the men tied his wrists. 'We don't have money.'

'Your friend isn't poor, is he?' Yung smirked. 'And I think you have something we want.'

Arky was about to ask more questions when the other man wrapped a thick tape over his mouth and gagged him. Then he was picked up, carried along a hallway and thrown into a room.

Arky landed heavily on someone who grunted loudly. He rolled off his victim and found himself face to face with Bear, who was also gagged.

Bear's face was turning deep red from the impact. Winded, his eyes bugged out and his chest heaved.

Finally, after several distressing moans, he sucked air through his nose. Colour came back to his face.

Arky widened his eyes at Bear, trying to apologise for hurting him.

Yung poked his toe into Bear's stomach. 'Suck it up, rich boy!' he said. 'Got yourself into a bit of trouble then!' He left their room, shutting and bolting a wooden door.

A scuffling came from behind Arky. He swivelled his head to see what was making the sound. Tue was gagged and bound, struggling against his bonds. He looked as scared as Arky felt. Arky frantically pulled and sawed his hands against his ropes, but only succeeded in bruising his wrists.

Tue shuffled to a sitting position under a small window and attempted to stand, using the wall for support. The window was small and high, letting in a dull light. Arky studied it, looking for a way to escape. It was unlocked.

He rolled onto his tummy, moving himself along the ground like a caterpillar towards Tue. As he inched forward, the tape over his mouth scraped against the ground. He had an idea. He rubbed his face back and forth on the dusty floor. A sneeze built up in his mouth and exploded through his nose. Snot spurted into the dirt, but the tape moved. Several seconds later, his chin sandpapered red, the tape rolled off. A fierce sense of victory encouraged him. Now they had a chance to escape!

Tue, seeing Arky's success, dropped to the ground and began rubbing his mouth on the floor. While Tue was busy, Arky shuffled up beside Bear. He pulled and chewed at the rope binding Bear's wrists. It took several minutes, but the rope loosened and Bear was free. He in turn undid Arky's and Tue's ties. Removing the tape from his mouth, Bear was about to speak, but Arky silenced him with a finger to his lips.

The boys moved under the window and sized it up. Being the skinniest, Arky thought he might possibly squeeze through.

Without a word, Tue reached up and opened the window. Bear knelt and Arky climbed on his back. Arky sucked his tummy in as he squeezed through the tiny opening. The wooden sill caught his hips. He pushed and pulled but he was stuck.

'Your hips are too big,' Bear whispered. 'You're stuck by your belt and jeans.'

Arky felt fingers pulling off his shoes, undoing his belt and hauling his jeans and his underpants off. Bare-bummed, he was stuck half in and half out of the window.

Now what? he thought, still struggling to squeeze through. *I'm seriously stuck!* Suddenly firm hands rammed him hard. Arky popped out of the window into a courtyard. He stood up, half naked, and looked around. It was a dead end! There were solid walls on all sides. There was one door but it led back into the building he had just come from. He had no choice but to open the door, go back into the house, and hope to find another way out.

With his hands shaking in terror, he opened the door and crept fearfully into the house. An empty hallway lay ahead with a door at the other end. He sneaked past a shelf that held the coil of rope and tape that had been used to bind him. On the floor of the hallway were some old flour sacks. He picked one up to hide his nakedness, but noticed it had little bugs crawling in the webbing. He dropped it. There was nowhere to hide either, so he tiptoed on towards the door. He opened it a crack and peered around.

Sitting at a table, with his back to Arky, was Fong. His red hair fell across his face. He was reading. In front of him were two doors. One was bolted. Arky knew Bear and Tue were behind it. The second was the way out. *How am I going to get past Fong?* Arky wondered, feeling very exposed.

Arky wasn't sure how he got the idea, as his brain was whirling with fright, but almost without thinking he crept back up the hall. He took the coil of rope from the shelf and measured it out. It was over two metres long. He tied a slipknot in one end, making a hangman's noose. He put the tape in his jacket pocket. Next he picked up one of the sacks from the floor. He put the noose around the mouth of the sack.

Tense with fear, he crept back. He opened the door. Fong didn't turn. Arky took a step into the room, hesitating a second, then he lifted the sack and noose and plunged them over Fong's head.

Fong instantly put his hands up to grab the bag. Arky quickly pulled the noose tight and wound the rest of the rope around Fong's hands, trapping them against his neck. Fong kicked out violently. The chair crashed backwards, hitting the floor with a loud bang. Fong's head bashed onto the tiles. He grunted loudly and went limp.

Arky froze. The noise would bring Yung and the other bad guys! There was only one way to escape—but he didn't dare run through the door in case he ran into them. He waited nervously. No one came. He couldn't believe his luck. Fong was the only guard.

Realising Fong had knocked himself out, Arky checked he was still breathing and then removed the rope and sack from his head. He taped Fong's eyes and mouth shut and bound his arms and legs securely to the chair with the rope.

Arky unbolted the prison door. Tue and Bear almost shouted with relief when they saw him, but Arky put his finger to his lips in a warning.

Terrified they'd be caught at any minute, they sprinted out the door to freedom.

It wasn't till after the boys had raced down the front stairs, dashed through the narrow alleys and hidden behind some stacked crates beside a shop that Bear suddenly doubled over laughing. Tue pointed at Arky and giggled. Arky looked down. His private bits were blue with the cold. He'd been so frightened during the escape he had forgotten about his pants.

It took several minutes for Tue and Bear to hunt around the street and find a discarded plastic bag. Arky tied it round his waist to cover himself, and with the other boys staying close beside him, they made their way through the streets and back to the hotel.

Race to the Temple

'*There* you are!' Is yelled as Arky, Bear and Tue raced into their hotel room. 'We've been frantic! When we got back, you were gone.'

Her shouting alerted Doc, who emerged from his room, clutching the box holding the key. 'We looked everywhere for you, then someone jammed a ransom note under my door! They wanted the key in return for your freedom.' Then he noticed Arky's lack of shoes and pants. 'What on earth happened to you?'

'We were kidnapped,' Bear explained breathlessly. 'We left the hotel. I forced Arky and Tue to come with me. But Arky saved us! It was Yung and Fong! They're part of a gang.'

'They must have followed us after we left the cave, and discovered what we found,' Arky said.

'And they'll come after us once they realise we've escaped!' Tue said.

'We should go to the police and report what's happened.' Doc looked worried. 'Then we hand over the key and leave Mongolia.'

'Yung said the police were scared of him.' Arky pulled spare clothes from his pack and dressed quickly.

'The police won't help us,' Bear agreed. 'These people are bullies. No one listens when I've been bullied at school. This is exactly the same. I don't want them to win.'

'It would be a shame if someone else got hold of the key and went to the temple,' Arky said, trying to persuade his father.

'We've already got the permit to visit the temple, and I know the Head of the Monastery . . .' Is looked hopefully at Doc. 'And we know from sad experience that sometimes the police are in the pay of artefact thieves. We don't want too many people knowing where we are going. If we hurry, we could drive straight up to the temple, have a look around and then leave the country.'

'Please!' Bear begged. 'I don't want to come this far and never know if we could have found the tomb. Once my mother hears about what's happened to us, she'll send me to a summer camp for sure!'

'And what about Tue?' Arky said. 'What'll happen to him if we just leave? His family could be in danger. We have to find where this key leads us!'

Doc's eyes held a twinkle that Arky had never seen before. 'You have thirty seconds to get in the car,' he said.

On the way to the temple, Doc drove past the government offices and stopped at a disposal store. 'I have to buy some breathing gear,' he said. 'If we do find the tomb, it could be dangerous inside. It'll have been closed for so long the air will be bad.' He climbed out of the car. 'I won't be long.'

As Doc dashed into the store, Bear and Arky noticed the local government building was new and looked very different from the old part of town. In front of the main building was a large black Mercedes with a chauffeur behind the wheel.

'That must belong to a very important person,' Tue said. Just then, a well-dressed man came down the marble steps from the building.

'I know him!' Bear cried out. 'That's Mr Rulec. He's always competing with my stepfather in business.'

'What sort of business?' Is asked from the front of the car.

'Everything,' Bear replied. 'Last year it was a takeover of an African agricultural company. We won. My stepfather was bragging about it. They fight at auctions over antiques and things. Rulec is always sucking up to my mother too.'

Another man rushed down the stairs after Rulec and handed him a briefcase. As Rulec was talking to the man, he turned and spotted Bear. Once he'd finished chatting, he strode over.

'Good morning, Belvedere.' Rulec smiled. 'What on earth are you doing way out here, and without your butler minding you?'

Rulec smoothed his thin hair when he saw Is in the front.

Arky thought his eyes were cold and calculating.

Bear hesitated before he spoke. 'I'm with my aunty,' he lied. 'She's taking us adventuring.'

'This couldn't be your famous mother's sister?' Rulec let his eyes travel over Is and he looked puzzled.

'No,' Bear said, avoiding Rulec's eyes. 'My *real* father's sister, I do have other family, you know.'

'My name is Goran Rulec and you'd be Professor Isobel Smythe, if I'm not mistaken.' Rulec leered at Is. 'I've seen your photo alongside articles you've written. I'm quite a keen collector of artefacts myself and I'm particularly looking for Asian bits and pieces with interesting history. We'd have a lot in common, I think. I didn't realise Belvedere was so well connected.'

'I'm a stepsister actually.' Is blushed. 'But I like to keep in touch with Bear.'

'Of course!' Rulec flashed his big teeth at Is. 'We must meet up for a drink. You're welcome to visit me at the villa I've rented—it's just out of town. I'm talking to the government about a new mine they're planning. I can also help them build new roads. Matter of fact, I have all sorts of friends you might like to meet.'

'We're just leaving, really.' Is had spotted Doc, who was carrying respirators and torches back to the car.

Rulec dug into his pocket and produced a card. 'Well, here are my details,' he said, eyeing off Doc's baggage. 'What on earth do you need with those, Doctor Steele? You're not planning to go down an old mine shaft or into a tomb, are you?'

Doc threw the equipment into the back of the car. 'Mr Rulec,' he said, ignoring the question. 'We met once before at Lord Wright's.' He pushed past Rulec, climbed into the driver's seat and started the engine. 'I'd love to stop and talk, but we're in a bit of hurry.'

As they drove off, Doc warned Is, 'He deals in antiquities but he's got a bad reputation. I'd never work for him, though there are plenty who would.'

'Rulec might have hired Yung and Fong from the beginning,' Arky said from the back.

'Rulec doesn't seem the sort of person who'd have children kidnapped,' said Is. 'You can't go around accusing someone just because we've had problems with those thieves.'

'I wouldn't trust him,' Tue said. 'He has a hungry smile.'

'We can't judge people by their smile either.' Is sounded cross. 'Could he really know why we are here?'

'He knew who you were,' Bear said. 'It was like he enjoyed pretending to be surprised I was here. He must have known my stepfather had bought the gold coin. And those two kinda hate each other!'

'He's just been in the government offices,' warned Doc. 'He would've learned about our permission to search the temple. It is possible he's behind what happened to us.'

'And he's got cars and planes and things,' Bear said, 'and he can have us followed really quickly.'

'Mmm,' murmured Is. 'Well, it won't help him because as soon as we return we are going to go to the local authorities and hand over the coin, the key and the location of the cave with the dead warriors in it. And then we're going home.'

Eyes Filled With Gold

The monks in the temple remembered Is from her last visit and welcomed everyone warmly. There were many gongs hanging from the walls and the monks were constantly ringing them so the building hummed with a gentle sound.

'Why are the monks ringing the gongs nine times?' Arky asked, trying to remember what Doc had said earlier about the number nine.

'Nine is a lucky number,' Doc said, 'and there are 999 gongs here. The monks believe ringing them reminds people of Buddha's enlightenment.'

'Wow.' Bear's voice was sarcastic. 'How's all this information useful?'

'If we know legends and history,' Doc said patiently, 'they will help us discover the clues left by the Keeper of Secrets.'

'When are we going to look under the monastery?' Arky wished they would hurry up.

'Is is checking with the abbot,' Doc said. 'She wants to make sure he is still happy for us to explore the catacomb underneath the temple.'

'Catacomb?' asked Tue.

'It's a series of underground rooms,' Doc replied. 'It's like a cemetery, but the monks are not buried. You can see their bodies in niches carved in the rock walls. They lie there until they rot. It can be a bit shocking at first.'

Minutes later, the abbot arrived. He nodded at the respirators they all carried. His eyes sparkled with amusement and he said something to Is, who smiled and translated. 'He said the dead are not that smelly! You can breathe down there without respirators.'

The abbot led them out through a garden to the back of the temple, then down a few stairs to an ancient door set into the massive foundations. The door opened to a long hall that echoed eerily with their footsteps. Arky and Bear were quiet, while Tue seemed slightly worried. Arky wondered if he was thinking about ghosts again, like he had been in the cave. Eventually, they came to a steep flight of stairs that disappeared into darkness. There was no electric light and at the top of the stairs an old bell hung suspended on a rope. Doc took torches out of his backpack. The abbot said something to Is and bowed.

'The abbot knows we have come to search for Genghis Khan's burial place,' she translated. 'He thinks we are wasting our time, and we won't find any secret tunnels. For hundreds of years the monks have explored every room down here . . . but he respects our right to see this world of the dead without his presence. He wishes us well and tells us to ring this bell when we have finished exploring.'

Once they were alone, Doc led the way down the stairs into the darkness. There was a musty smell that became stronger as they went down. Finally they found themselves in a long dark room lined with carved holes in the walls.

Lying in the niches were the bodies of monks, wearing stained orange robes. Some still had flesh clinging to their skulls. Arky's nose wrinkled at the rotting smell and he tried not to look at the corpses. Bear was muttering under his breath and waving his torch around to highlight the dead. Doc gave him a bop on the head to remind him about his manners.

Bear couldn't handle being told off. As they continued through the suffocating catacombs, he spotted a room off to one side—full of monks sitting in stone chairs—and ducked away to explore.

He brushed a cobweb off his face and something moved in his hair. He put up his hand. A squashy, furry body wriggled under his fingers. He yelped in fright and hit at the repulsive creature as it ran down his brow, its enormous black body hanging over one of his eyes.

'Spider!' he screamed. The spider scuttled down his nose, dropped to his neck and ran under his clothes.

Waving his torch, he tried pulling off his jumper. As his jumper went over his head, the spider ran across his tummy. Bear crashed blindly into one of the sitting corpses. Bones and fragments of clothing flew into the air.

Doc raced to Bear's side and pulled him upright. He tore off Bear's jumper and brushed the spider away. It darted into the darkness. 'You stupid boy!' Doc growled. 'What will the monks say when they see this?'

'We've got to put the bones back!' Is said. 'And you've wasted our time!'

Gently, Doc and Is placed the monk back on his chair and settled his head back on his shoulders. They had to leave his arms on the floor because they were no longer held in place by the robes. 'I'll explain to the abbot later,' Is said, looking concerned. 'Please try and control yourself, Bear. We're almost in the last room, so stay beside me!'

She walked away, followed by a guilty-looking Bear, down a narrow corridor towards a darkened archway, almost hidden in the gloom. They ducked through it and disappeared into another chamber.

❖

When Bear gave a stifled cry, Arky hurriedly followed inside. His torch lit up a mound of bones and skulls piled higher than his head. And then the light fell on another, and another.

'What is this?' Arky shuddered.

'Don't be scared,' Is said. 'When the monks in the catacombs fall to pieces, their bones are moved into this vault. You are looking at hundreds of years of dead monks.'

'Look!' Arky pointed to a wall covered with carved skulls with gaping jaws. 'All the eye sockets are filled with gold!'

'It's like they're watching us,' whispered Bear, awed. 'The torchlight makes their eyes glitter. It's spooky.'

'*Very* spooky,' added Tue. 'I really do not want to be here.' He stood as close to the entrance as possible.

'Traitors!' Is cried. 'Traitors discovered by the Hand of Death were killed by pouring gold into their eyes!'

'That's disgusting!' Bear said.

'It is a clue,' Is continued, 'to remind the searchers that we are looking for the Hand of Death.'

'How will we find it?' Bear trembled slightly. 'Do we have to move more bones?'

Arky waved his torch around. He noticed that the other three walls in the vault were brightly decorated like the Buddha's feet upstairs in the hall. Animals, flowers, birds, flowing streams and mountains filled every centimetre. The walls would have been beautiful if they were in any other room.

'The paintings are of paradise,' Doc said, following Arky's torchlight.

'The skulls are only on one wall,' Arky said, thoughtfully. 'It's another clue.'

'You're right!' Is exclaimed. 'The traitors are all carved on the east wall! And that's wrong. In

Chinese mythology, death is always shown on the west, where the sun goes down. That's where these carved death heads should be. And because they're only carvings, not real skulls, they are not real death. We need to look at the west wall for *real* death!'

'The entrance to the tomb will be on the west wall.' Doc smiled. 'And Genghis will be in paradise!'

Everyone shone their torches on the west wall and examined the paintings. Within seconds, Arky had spotted a dragon with a big smile on its face. The smile was carved into the rock, not painted like all the other pictures. He moved carefully around a pile of bones and touched the dragon. It was the same dragon that was on the cover of Tue's book, but without a pearl in its mouth. He fingered the mouth. There was a slit that went quite deep into the rock.

'If you poked the big circle of the key into this mouth,' he said thoughtfully, 'then it would look like this dragon had a pearl in its mouth.'

Doc moved like lightning. Without asking, he took Is's backpack, undid the clasp and pulled out the key. Within seconds the grooved rim of the key was in the dragon's mouth.

'Now what?' asked Bear. 'It looks pretty, but it's not doing anything.'

'Push,' urged Is. 'It fits, so you either have to push or turn. It must do something!'

'I don't want to bend it,' Doc said, pushing the key into the wall.

Seconds ticked by.

'Nothing!' said Doc, his shoulders drooping. 'I'll pull it out.'

As he pulled the key out, a weird 'click' came from deep inside the room. Everyone held their breath as a low rumble shook the west wall. A faint crack appeared near the dragon and grew bigger until Arky could see the outline of a doorway.

Doc and Is pushed against the rocky door with all their might. Finally it gave way and crashed open. A cloud of vapour gushed into the room. Arky held his breath, but the oppressive smell of death, sour and acidic, caught his nostrils.

'Into the shadow of death,' whispered Bear.

The Sound
of Enlightenment

Doc passed Arky the key and handed out the breathing equipment. Arky put the key in his backpack and lifted the heavy respirator onto his head. His breath came hard and raspy, filling the crypt with an eerie rattling. The glass in front of his face misted over for a few seconds before it cleared. He took his first step into the tomb and jumped with fright as an enormous soldier, clutching a huge sword, loomed in front of him.

It took him a few seconds to realise the soldier was a statue. It had hideous bulging eyes, giant fangs and pig-like ears. Behind the first monster were more than forty of the large statues, all guarding the way to an immense treasure.

'These are spirit guards,' Doc said, as the boys stared at the statues in awe. 'They protect the dead.'

'What a nightmare!' Bear shuddered.

'Look up,' Tue said, shining his torch on the roof. Above him, the roof glittered like a starry night. Hundreds of crystals were set into the roof.

'This is the tomb,' Arky said. 'But where's Genghis?'

Tue's torchlight pointed to the centre of the vast room, highlighting a large golden box. 'There!' he said.

'Incredible!' Is rushed towards the glittering coffin.

'I want you boys to stay put,' Doc said, but his voice rose with excitement. 'Don't touch anything!' He headed after Is.

Arky almost tripped on the uneven floor near the spirit guards as he turned to let his torch play over the vastness of the tomb. His beam lit a three-dimensional model of China and Mongolia. It was several metres square. The mountains glittered with quartz and jade, carved to perfection. The rivers were silver, the lakes made of poisonous mercury.

On the other side of the model lay rows of fallen soldiers wearing fine armour. They reclined in perfect peace in a well-designed pattern.

'They must be the 999 soldiers the Keeper of Secrets poisoned.' Arky was fascinated by the gruesome sight. 'The men who carried Genghis to his tomb!'

'Nine rows of dead men,' Bear said, walking up and down beside them. He looked around the enormous tomb. 'But how are we going to find the Hand of Death among all these other treasures?'

'The Keeper of Secrets was very clever,' Tue said. 'He would have left us a clue.'

Arky thought for a moment, and then he laughed. 'He *did*. Remember when we looked at your book, the temple had gongs drawn around it?'

Tue nodded.

'So?' asked Bear.

'The gongs wouldn't have been drawn there for nothing.'

'So the first to the gong wins the prize,' Bear said, leaping into the gloom.

Tue smiled and took off to hunt for their clue. Doc's and Is's torchlights were a long way back in the tomb as the boys began their search. Arky wondered briefly if he should call them over and tell them about the gong idea, but his thoughts were cut short as Bear gave a low whistle.

Beside the fallen soldiers and behind a large column decorated with birds and flowers, Bear had found a golden gong. It hung from wires connected to hooks set in the ceiling.

'Should I ring it?' Bear asked, as Tue joined them.

'I wouldn't,' advised Arky. 'Doc said not to touch anything.'

'Ringing isn't touching.' With a wicked grin, Bear hit the gong with the back of his torch. The gong rang out and echoed loudly. 'Nine times!' cried Bear, beating the gong hard and fast.

The wires in the gong vibrated and shimmered. The sound it made was deafening. Dust fell from the ceiling. Then both wires broke. The gong clattered to the ground.

The hooks in the roof made a groaning sound and rotated. Inside the column decorated with birds and flowers, a small door clicked open, revealing a cupboard.

Arky shone his torch towards it and the boys peered inside. It was empty. The walls were painted completely black, except for three gold characters that stood out at the back.

'Nine. Nine. Nine,' said Tue, reading the symbols. 'The number of dragons in my book and the number for the Khan.'

'How does that help?' Bear seemed disappointed.

'It does!' Arky said. 'Look. It is nine with a space and then two nines together. At school we did the library code. It's an easy way to hide a message. You go to shelf nine and down ninety-nine books.'

'So?' said Bear, who now looked a little worried because Doc and Is were striding towards him. Even through their respirators they appeared very angry.

'You said there were nine rows of dead soldiers!' Tue said, getting the idea first. 'We go to the last row and count down ninety-nine men!'

Doc and Is weren't angry at all once they realised what Bear had discovered. Together, they went to row nine and their torchlight glittered over the ninety-ninth man. His armour was covered in dragons with precious stones set in their eyes. His shield was a coiled golden dragon with a pearl in its mouth. One of his arms was covered in chain-mail armour, and at the end of it was a steel glove. The other hand was exposed and the bones gleamed white.

Doc carefully pulled at the armoured hand.

'Only one of his arms is real!' Tue said, as the armour came off easily. Doc held the heavy hand up and undid the glove. Inside was a skeletal hand made of gold. Each nail was forged sharp and long, like a tiger's claw. One finger pointed outwards accusingly.

There was a small gold pin underneath so the hand would spin.

All at once they exclaimed, 'The Hand of Death!'

Doc carefully put the hand back in the glove, and placed it in his backpack. 'This is one treasure we have to keep to ourselves till we talk to Lord Wright,' he said. 'It's time we went up and told the monks about our discovery.'

The words were barely out of his mouth when a loud noise made them turn. Two men burst into the tomb. They carried high-powered spotlights that cut through the gloom like a knife. As Arky swung his torch towards them, a gun fired. The bullet whizzed past Arky's head, ricocheted off the wall behind him and pinged backwards. One of the intruders yelped loudly as the bullet narrowly missed his head.

'Turn your torches off!' Doc ordered Is and the boys. 'Drop to the floor.'

'Give up and you'll live!' called a voice.

'That's Yung,' Arky said. 'I recognise his voice.'

'They're wearing respirators,' Doc said. 'There's only one way they could've known they were needed.'

'Rulec!' Bear said. 'He must have told Yung and given him a car to chase us.'

'Can we get past them?' Arky asked.

'We'll try,' replied Doc. 'I'll crawl away closer to the coffin and make a noise. When they come after me, you all make a dash for the door.'

While Doc felt his way through the darkness, the tomb raiders made their way further into the tomb, raking ahead with their spotlights.

Something crashed to the ground near Genghis's coffin and the tomb echoed with the clatter. The raiders swung their spotlights towards the sound and the golden casket lit up. It glittered invitingly. The tomb raiders stopped and stared. They took a few steps towards the sarcophagus. 'You can't escape!' Yung yelled.

'You'll have to get us first,' Doc called, his voice sounding ghostly from the darkness.

The tomb raiders swept the air with their fierce lights and continued into the crypt.

Is and the boys moved behind them, tiptoeing towards the secret door. They were almost there when Arky stumbled and crashed into one of the statues. Arky held his breath while the spirit guard tottered and then, to his horror, it fell and thudded into Is. A massive boom echoed throughout the tomb as the statue landed and pinned Is to the ground.

Arky rushed to Is's side as she let out a painful gasp from under the statue. She was badly winded so Arky grabbed her arms and tried to pull her free, but the statue was too heavy.

Tue and Bear quickly rushed over to help. They didn't have much time—the tomb raiders' lights swept towards them. Straining, the three of them managed to lift the statue. Just as Is wriggled free, the raiders spotlighted them. Arky froze next to Bear and Tue, blinking under the blazing lights, wondering what to do.

Doc made a lot of noise not too far away and one of the men was distracted and turned back into the tomb. The other man, spotlight wavering, charged towards Is as she tried to get to her feet. He was on them in seconds. There was a flash of a knife as it was thrust towards Is's throat.

Without thinking, Arky leapt onto the man's back. Arky's attack pushed him sideways and his spotlight skittered away into the darkness and went out.

Not knowing what to do next, and realising the man might use his knife, Arky wrenched at the man's respirator. To his surprise it came off. The man gagged, dropped his knife and thrashed wildly at Arky, trying to get the respirator back.

Arky leapt out of his way, fell and rolled into the dark. The man, gasping for breath, went after him. Arky kept rolling.

'You're dead!' Yung's voice came to Arky from the back of the tomb. His spotlight spun in the direction of their scuffle. It lit his friend, who had fallen and was gasping for air. 'Give the respirator back!'

Arky stumbled to his feet still gripping the stolen respirator. Yung was instantly beside him. He made a grab for Arky, but as his other hand was holding his spotlight he wasn't as quick as he hoped.

Arky leapt backwards. Yung grabbed one of Arky's legs. Arky kicked but Yung hung on.

As Arky tried to shake him free, Bear and Tue leapt from the darkness to help. Bear threw himself at Yung's feet while Tue launched at his head. Yung crashed to the ground with a grunt under the weight of the two boys. Bear grabbed the spotlight and hurled it into the darkness. There was a smashing of glass and its light died. Tue, clinging like a monkey to Yung's head, pulled off his respirator.

As Yung choked on the foul air, the boys scrambled away, holding the captured respirators. Doc, now using his flashlight, raced to join them and dragged Is to her feet. They ran for the door, as Yung, gasping for breath, pulled his gun from his belt.

Shots exploded against the wall as the team dashed through the secret door. Tue hauled the door shut behind them, trapping the attackers inside the tomb.

Arky rang the bell for all he was worth.

In search of help, Doc and Is dashed through the garden towards the temple's main hall. The monks, who were peacefully at prayer, were very surprised when they burst in. The tomb was so far below that they hadn't heard the noise.

Once Is explained what had happened, the abbot led the monks down to the catacombs. Doc showed them the secret door. The monks were clearly concerned. The abbot spoke to Is.

'They're worried about the wellbeing of the men inside, even though Yung has a gun,' Is explained. 'We must get them out!'

'Arky, get the key out of your pack,' Doc ordered. 'These men may be bad but we don't want them to die.'

Arky put the key in the dragon's mouth and pulled it out again. The monks muttered in bewilderment as the door opened, and Yung and his friend staggered out. Wheezing, tears running down their faces, they fell at the abbot's feet. The monks lost no time in removing their weapons and binding them.

'We'll fix you!' wheezed Yung, glaring at the boys, as he was marched away by the monks.

'I don't know how he'll do that.' Bear smiled at Arky. 'He'll be in jail very soon, I should think.'

Arky and Bear were kept busy the day after finding the tomb. The police took statements from them about the kidnapping and Yung's raid on the tomb. Yung and his sidekick were charged with kidnapping, theft and attempted murder.

'What about Fong?' Arky asked. 'Won't he come after us?'

'I don't think so,' the policeman replied. 'It is too dangerous in town now. I should think he and his gang are long gone.'

Arky wondered if the policeman was telling the truth, and if the police would hunt for the rest of

Yung's gang or try to discover how they knew about their expedition to the temple. Even though Doc had locked the Hand of Death in a safety deposit box in the bank in town, and kept the key with him at all times, Arky was sure they hadn't heard the last of Fong.

The Last Clue in
the Book

In a private mansion on the outskirts of Ulaangom, Rulec paced up and down. He held a copy of the local English-language newspaper with the headline: 'Genghis Khan's Tomb Found'. A front-page picture of Lord Wright made Rulec grind his teeth.

Wright had won again! Rulec slammed the paper down on the floor. *Wright must have a weakness*, he thought.

He picked up the phone and dialled the direct line of a local minister.

'Mr Batukhan,' he said. 'I hear Genghis Khan's tomb has been discovered. I also understand Lord

Wright is going to visit the tomb. As you know, I am very fond of historical artworks and I've donated generously to your election campaign. I would take it as a personal favour to be there at the same time as Lord Wright.'

He smiled when he hung up. He would enjoy the look on Wright's face when he discovered he no longer had a private viewing of the tomb.

The phone rang again. It was that fool Fong.

'I told you to only contact me if there's an emergency,' Rulec hissed. 'Your brother messed things up. So far you've brought me nothing but trouble. You have one more chance to get things right or your brother can rot.'

'What do you want me to do?' Fong sounded upset. 'I want to free my brother.'

'I need to know what's going on,' Rulec said. 'I want the professor's and Doctor Steele's rooms bugged. I don't want to miss a word they say to each other. Get me some good information and I may be able to help with your problem. Tell your brother not to talk.'

The boys were allowed back into the tomb after it was fitted with special lights that didn't hurt the old treasures, and so researchers and historians could photograph and record everything inside.

Being in the tomb was awesome. Wonderful woven rugs and inlaid furniture were arranged to resemble sumptuous lounge rooms and bedrooms. Sculptures and paintings of beautiful women lay against walls. Barrels of wine and food, stored for Genghis to eat in his afterlife, were stacked near a table heaped with golden plates, cups and chopsticks.

Along with the rows of dead soldiers, and their armour and weapons, were marble and terracotta statues of people cooking, riding horses, sewing and gardening. The walls of the tomb were carved and painted with stories of Genghis's life and his many battles.

The boys spent hours studying the wild horses, the angry faces of the soldiers and the terror-filled faces of their victims. Best of all, they were allowed to see into Genghis's sarcophagus.

Arky held his breath as he stepped up and peered inside. The interior was lined with red cloth. Lying in a wrapping of stained golden silk was the long rotted body of the Khan. Arky let his eyes travel up to the famous king's skull. Grey hair still clung to his cranium and shrivelled flaking skin covered his cheekbones. His yellowed teeth grinned up at them, and Arky thought he looked surprisingly cheerful.

Tue, leaning over the ancient corpse, made a small sound in the back of his throat, and his eyes grew wider. 'This is my ancestor!' he gasped.

Bear placed a hand on Tue's shoulder. 'Amazing,' he agreed.

'He always wanted a descendant to find his tomb,' Doc said, 'and it has happened.'

'He has many, many descendants these days,' Tue said, proudly. 'And now he can help us all.'

❖

While everyone waited for Lord Wright to arrive, the boys enjoyed a little notoriety. Whenever they left the hotel room, people smiled at them or patted them on the back. They grinned happily, proud of their success.

Bear had plenty of time to use his credit card, and bought a new computer and mobile phone. He also made sure they feasted on pies, cakes and sweets until Tue, who had never had such sugary goodies before, ate far too much and vomited all over the hotel carpet.

Once Bear's stepfather finally landed in his private helicopter in Ulaangom, Doc drove out to meet him with Bear and Arky. When Lord Wright stepped out of the helicopter and shook Doc's hand, Arky couldn't help but compare the two men.

Lord Wright was tall and slightly flabby around the middle, but handsome. He had thick dark hair, white film star teeth and flashing green eyes. Doc, on the other hand, was shorter, more ordinary looking and slightly stooped from years of poring over books. But Doc was well-muscled, not flabby like Lord Wright. Arky smiled. Doc had to be fit or else he'd never keep up with Arky's mum when they went on holidays. He wondered how Alice was going in Alaska and if she'd heard about their success yet or if she was high on a remote peak away from all the news.

Lord Wright walked confidently over to the boys and put his hand on Bear's shoulder. 'I hope you weren't too troublesome,' he said, looking stern.

Bear lifted his head high and didn't reply.

Lord Wright turned to Arky. 'You've done your father proud,' he said.

Bear's eyes flashed with annoyance at the comment and his face reddened. Arky was about to say that they couldn't have done anything without Bear, when Lord Wright turned his back on the boys, addressing Doc. 'I understand you have something you want to talk privately about.'

'We'll talk back at the hotel,' Doc replied. 'I have a couple of surprises I want to show you.'

❖

'It's amazing,' Lord Wright cried, turning the Hand of Death over and over. The boys, Doc and Is had expected him to be angry that they hadn't told him about it earlier, but he looked pleased.

'I haven't given the Hand of Death to the government because I think we might need it to unlock the next clue,' Doc said. 'The boys found the hand by solving the riddles in Tue's ancient Book of Clues. The Keeper of Secrets said we needed the Book of Clues to find the tomb and Genghis Khan's lost treasure.'

'And you think this artefact will help you find his treasure?' Lord Wright stroked the long fingernails on the hand. 'The workmanship is stunning,' he muttered.

'We think the Book of Clues led us to the hand specifically so, in turn, I believe we will need the hand to help us solve another riddle or puzzle.' Doc turned, picked up Tue's book and brought it over. 'But we can't let anyone know about the Book of Clues or the Hand of Death just yet. Not till we work out why we need the hand.'

'I understand.' Lord Wright nodded. 'There are some in the government who aren't that trustworthy. We don't want this treasure taken by thieves and treasure hunters.' He looked expectantly at Doc. 'So what is the next clue?'

Doc put the Book of Clues on Lord Wright's lap. 'Isobel is the only one who can read it.'

'And I have no idea.' Is sighed. 'I've read it several times, but I can't find anything that mentions the hand or how we can use it to solve a puzzle that will lead us to the legendary treasure.'

'Maybe you've looked too hard,' Arky suggested. 'Perhaps we should look in the Book of Clues for words like "death" and "hand", but not the actual Hand of Death. There may even be a clue about where we should go next.'

Is nodded. 'It's good idea,' she said. 'Only the last story in the book mentions the words "hand" and "death", but I can't see a clue in it at all.'

They crowded around Lord Wright as he turned the pages slowly, till he came to the last page. A king with a fine jewelled crown, wearing a leopard cloak around his shoulders, was painted across two pages. The king aimed his bow and arrow at a leopard standing proudly on a snow-covered rock.

'Read it to us,' Arky begged.

'There was once a king of the mountains,' read Is. 'He went hunting. When he saw a leopard he took aim, but the leopard waited for the arrow to claim its life. "Aren't you afraid of *death*?" asked the king. "Why do you stand like stone?"

'The leopard said, "You own all things, my lord. My life is yours."

'The king replied, "I stay my *hand*. Go and live. Ye shall be king of the mountains and wear the crown upon my orders. And only the lord Buddha will see where ye are, and in time ye shall be king."'

'That's it?' asked Bear. 'No more pages or pictures?'

'Nothing more,' Is said. 'The words "hand" and "death" appear, but it makes no sense to me.'

'The king is wearing a crown and a leopard cloak . . .' Doc said.

'So,' asked Bear, 'where is this leading?'

'Did you notice that Genghis Khan wasn't wearing a crown when you opened his coffin?' Arky asked. 'Wouldn't you think he'd be buried with his crown?'

'I don't know,' Is replied. 'But you are right—there wasn't a crown in Genghis's sarcophagus.'

'Then where is it?' Arky felt a rush of energy.

'Is the crown the next clue?' asked Bear.

'It could be.' Doc sounded thoughtful.

'So this story might be telling us where the crown is hidden,' Bear said. 'It is a clue to where to look. Do we look for a leopard?'

'Is there a *leopard* anything nearby?' asked Lord Wright, becoming excited.

Bear took out his new mobile phone, connected to the internet and opened up a map of Mongolia. Everyone crowded around him as his screen showed the world turning and slowly getting closer and closer to where they were staying. 'Leopard Mountain,' Bear said, looking at the map of Mongolia. 'There's a Leopard Mountain in the national park near this town.'

'It says, "stand like stone" and "king of the mountains" in the Book of Clues,' Arky said excitedly. 'It fits. I think we're onto something.'

Bear googled the national park and came up with more information. 'It says it's very steep, covered in snow and dangerous to climb.'

'I know there is an old abandoned Buddhist hermitage up in that national park,' Is said. 'It's full of Buddha carvings in the cliffs. I've read about it, and seen pictures, but it is not very famous. It would fit with the words, "the Lord Buddha will see where ye are". The hermits moved out long ago. The big carvings are crumbling into ruin, but I don't know if the hermitage is at Leopard Mountain.'

'There is only one way to find out if your guesses are right,' said Arky, 'and that's to go and look.'

'It's deep in the mountains,' Doc said. 'There are no roads. We could never trek that far without a team of sherpas to help us.'

'You have a helicopter,' Bear said, staring at his stepfather. 'You could take Doc up there and *you* could look around.'

Lord Wright thought for a moment, weighing up the situation. Finally he said, 'I can't go, but the chopper would give you a chance to get away from any thugs who might still be trying to follow you. If the crown's at Leopard Mountain, then you could be dropped as close as possible. The helicopter could come back and pick you up a few days later. Would that give you enough time?'

Doc nodded. 'If the chopper could get us close, Is and I could walk in. We could take two days to search the old ruins. Then walk out. We would need six days, just in case the track was steeper than we expected and we had to slow down a bit.'

'I would like to go,' said Is, 'but I'm responsible for so much work at the tomb. If I disappeared it would cause suspicion. You could go, Doc. We could say you're going to do some research for another job for Lord Wright.'

'Couldn't *we* go?' pleaded Arky. 'We're only small, and we've helped heaps with everything so far.'

'If you come back with Genghis Khan's crown, then it will be a bonus,' said Lord Wright, ignoring

Arky's plea. 'Rulec doesn't know about the hand and our hunt for the next clue to lead us to the treasure. I'll keep him busy here. You should be safe.'

'But can *we* go?' asked Arky again.

Lord Wright looked critically at Bear. 'I've been hearing more about your adventures. It seems you've been helpful. What do you think, Doc?'

Doc's eyes twinkled. 'I suppose three boys don't weigh much and would fit in the helicopter!'

The Crown of
the Ruler

It didn't take long for Doc to organise backpacks, hiking gear and rations, and find a detailed map of Leopard Mountain. A few days later, while Lord Wright and Rulec were visiting Genghis Khan's tomb, the helicopter landed on a small knoll on the lower slopes of the mountain.

The boys and Doc clambered down from the cabin and shouldered their packs. The pilot winked, the rotor blades whirred, and the chopper took off, buffeting them with its downdraft.

Within an hour, Arky was covered in sweat and his pack was digging into his back. The winding trail up to the Buddhist hermitage was more of a climb than a walk. Bear made good time, keeping ahead of Arky. Arky noticed Bear was a lot fitter than when they had first met.

Tue was very excited about having special hiking boots, plus clothes, a backpack and Gore-Tex jacket. He walked so fast that even Doc couldn't keep up with him. 'Slow down!' Doc ordered. 'It's not a race and we have to keep together.'

They plodded onwards and upwards, steadily climbing into a steep ravine.

'Time for a rest,' Doc called, seeing Arky struggling under the weight of his pack. 'We can't stop for too long though. We could get an early snowfall.' He pointed to the steep mountain above them. Already snow clouds were forming on its icy peak.

A short time later, while walking through a fog drifting with snowflakes, Arky thought he heard a pounding noise. 'Is that our helicopter?' he asked, stopping. 'Has it come back?'

Doc twisted his head to listen. 'I can hear something too.' He turned and looked back the way they had come, trying to pinpoint the noise, but the sound had vanished. He shrugged his shoulders. 'It might have been the echo of a rock falling.'

They soon forgot about the odd noise as they climbed past little piles of rocks. The cairns were marked with tattered prayer flags. When night fell, they made camp on a steep slope and hammered their tent pegs into the rock.

The following day, the track grew steeper and more slippery. Bear fell once and bruised his knee. Tue helped him up and took his pack until Bear stopped limping.

By the time they reached the long-abandoned hermitage, every muscle in Arky's body was aching. He was almost too tired to admire the five large buddhas carved into the mountain.

'They must be more than ten metres high!' Bear exclaimed. 'And look at all the little caves around them.'

'That's where the hermits lived,' Doc explained. 'They carved the buddhas. Some say they didn't sleep for years at a time or talk to anyone.'

'How did they carve everything so high into the cliff?' Bear asked.

Doc pointed at a section of rock. 'They chipped away at the cliff and probably made wooden platforms to stand on. You'll find tunnels running inside the mountain like rabbit warrens, as well as little caves that were used as windows, and nooks where they slept.'

'Which buddha is hiding the crown?' Arky wondered aloud.

'I'd look in the biggest one,' Bear suggested.

'In the morning.' Doc smiled. 'You boys must be exhausted. How about we camp in that large cave between the biggest buddha's feet tonight? It'll be warm in there.'

Despite his aching muscles, Arky spent several minutes exploring the cave. He half-expected a hermit to appear because everything inside the cave seemed brand new. Firewood was placed against a wall and some cooking pots and several empty sleeping nooks were nearby.

The explorers made good use of the wood and had a blaze crackling merrily in the fireplace.

Arky pulled out his sleeping bag and happily watched the flickering firelight in the vast cavern. His last memory was of the painted gods on the ceiling smiling down on him.

When he awoke, Doc was squatting by the fire and breakfast was ready. 'I've been into a few of the caves and tunnels in this buddha already this morning,' he said, while the boys were eating. 'They get narrower and smaller as they go up, but I haven't found anything yet.'

After breakfast they began exploring. Some tunnels went on for ages before they found out they went nowhere and had wasted valuable time.

Finally, towards late afternoon, and after many false leads, only one passageway around the big buddha was left to explore. They followed the passageway up and up as it grew smaller and even Arky had to stoop to get through. Eventually it opened out into a cave near the buddha's shoulders.

Light flooded into the tunnel but the way ahead was even narrower and they would have to crawl.

Doc had to stop. 'It's too narrow for me,' he puffed, removing his backpack. 'Here, you take the Hand of Death and see if you can get through to the statue's head.'

Arky took the treasure and the boys scrambled upwards. 'The hermits must have been skinny little guys,' Bear said, squeezing through a narrow burrow.

Seconds later they found themselves in a large room carved into the rock behind the buddha's eyes. A weak afternoon light came in through the buddha's pupils. Arky went to one and looked out through the buddha's eye. A light snowfall was filling the valley. 'Awesome,' he said.

Tue laughed. 'What would my parents say if I told them I stood in God's head!'

'And *this* is awesome,' called Bear, making his friends turn. 'The same picture as in Tue's book is painted on this wall! Look!'

Sure enough, there was a large painting of the king standing beside a spotted leopard. He was wearing a crown and leopard cloak. The painting was on the back wall so the light from the buddha's eyes would shine on the ancient artwork.

'We have to be close to finding the crown.' Bear stood in front of the painting.

'Like in the temple,' Arky suggested. 'We should study the painting for a secret door or something different.'

Bear was quick to find what they were looking for. 'Here,' he cried, poking his finger into a hole in one of the leopard's spots.

'And the finger of the hand will fit inside it.' Arky smiled. 'Like the rim of the key fitted in the dragon's mouth.'

Arky pulled off his pack and took out the Hand of Death. The sunlight glittered on the gold as he pushed the finger into the leopard's spot. He pressed his weight against the hand. There was a loud click. A small door opened, revealing a compartment.

Inside was a golden crown. The years hadn't dulled it. Rubies glittered in the band. Four pearl-encrusted arches rose to the centre, supporting a spike topped with an enormous crystal.

The boys stared in awe at their find.

'Should we pick it up?' Tue whispered.

'It's kinda yours,' Bear said, standing back and letting Tue pick the crown up.

'Your ancestor wore it, so you should,' Bear said.

Tue lifted it up and put the crown on his head. It slipped, falling onto his ears and pushing them down. He went proudly over to the buddha's eye-shaped windows. The sun glittered on the crown's stones, casting red rays around the room. 'I feel like a king right now.'

'You don't look like one.' Bear laughed. 'You look silly.'

Tue pulled the crown from his head, releasing his ears. He held the treasure to the light and the boys crowded around, inspecting it more closely.

'It's disappointing that the big crystal in the middle doesn't sparkle,' Bear said. 'You'd expect it to be a diamond, wouldn't you?'

Arky noticed the crystal was in two parts, held together with gold clasps and a gold knob at the top. 'I know I shouldn't . . . ' he said, reaching for the knob and turning it. As he had hoped, the knob was like a screw. It moved. The crystal separated, as if he had cut through a bubble. Inside the hollow was a round pink rock carved with tiny buddhas.

'It's carved so it looks like a walnut,' Bear observed, as Arky held the ornament in his hand. 'What kind of stone is it? Is it quartz?'

'Who knows, could be pink jade,' replied Arky, 'but it has to be the next clue to the treasure.'

'Doc'll know,' Tue said, with confidence. 'Let's give the crown to him.'

Arky put the pink ornament in his pocket and they returned through the narrow tunnels. Doc was waiting anxiously for them at the cave near the buddha's sholder. 'Amazing,' he said when they showed him the crown. He took a moment to study the crystals and rubies while Bear and Tue told him about the picture on the wall.

'We have to keep moving,' Doc said, 'it's getting dark.' With Doc proudly holding the crown, and Arky carrying the hand, they hurried back to their camp.

On the way, Arky had to stop for a leak. As Doc and the others stepped into the dying light of the painted cavern where they had made their camp, they froze. Fong and another man were standing by their campfire, pointing handguns at them.

'Move,' ordered Fong, his eyes lighting up at the sight of the crown in Doc's arms. He shook his gun, pointing for Doc, Tue and Bear to move to the doorway so he could see them better.

'How nice,' he said, holding the gun steady at Doc's chest. 'You have brought us a crown. I assume you still have the Hand of Death?'

Doc held the crown tightly to his chest and shook his head.

'Give up the Hand of Death and the Crown of the Great Khan.' Fong's voice grew angry. 'Or I will shoot.' His eyes narrowed.

Arky emerged from the tunnel and took in the situation at once. He ducked back into the shadows. His face flamed with rage as the second man approached his father and put the gun to his head.

Doc reluctantly gave up the crown. 'Now the hand,' ordered Fong.

'I don't know what you are talking about,' Doc said, seeing Arky behind Fong's accomplice. Doc stepped backwards, as if he were trying to escape, hoping to distract Fong so he wouldn't turn.

Fong stepped forwards. 'Don't you move again!' He turned his gun on Bear. 'I can shoot a kid as easy as you.'

Arky didn't know what to do. He could run and hide or he could try to save everyone. Both men held guns. Fong was closest to his father. The other man was just in front of Arky. He wore a heavy pack and looked strong.

'The hand!' Fong said. 'Where is it?'

Arky thought of the cruel nail on the hand's long, pointing finger. It was heavy and sharp. He pulled it from his pack, wondering if he could use it to knock the gun from the man in front of him. He had surprise on his side, and the man had a weak spot below his pack. If Arky caused a disturbance his dad might get the gun off Fong.

'Where's the little kid?' asked Fong, suddenly realising one person was missing.

Arky had no time to think further. He charged, holding the hand like a spear. He rammed it hard into the man's backside. The finger went deep. The man screamed. His gun flew into the air. But the man was tough. He spun around, grabbed the hand and pulled it from Arky's grasp. Arky fell flat on his face, then he pulled himself to his feet and looked around.

He had failed. Fong still had his gun pointed at Doc, and now both men stared murderously at him.

The hurt man limped to his gun and aimed it at Arky. He cocked the trigger. Arky shut his eyes, waiting for death.

'Shooting's too good for them,' Fong said. 'They will pay for this. We will make them suffer before they die.' He pointed his gun at their supplies. The second man, rubbing his bum, smiled as he worked out what Fong had in mind.

With guns at their heads, the boys were lined up against a wall while Doc was forced to gather their packs, food and sleeping bags and throw them onto the fireplace.

When everything they owned was in the pile, Fong ordered Doc to stand beside the boys.

'Now strip!' Fong said. 'Throw everything forward, one piece at a time.'

Arky's heart pounded with frustration as he took off his shoes and trousers and threw them over. Fong searched them, throwing them onto the pile. *I can't let them have everything,* Arky thought. *How will I hide the pink carving?* As he began to take off his jacket, he palmed the trinket.

He acted shy when he took off his underpants. He shuffled uncomfortably as he pulled them around his ankles.

'Skinny white legs.' Fong laughed, noticing Arky's behaviour.

Arky pretended to trip over his undies. Fong grinned as Arky fell flat on his back. While picking himself up, Arky pushed the carving into the dust built up against the cavern's wall.

Bear gave Arky an odd look when the carving wasn't discovered in his clothes.

Then Fong forced Doc to load the last of their wood on top of everything they owned. The second man, now hobbling painfully, removed a bottle from his pack and poured something over the pile. The smell of lighter fluid filled their nostrils. Fong laughed as he lit a match and threw it at the pile. Flames exploded.

Tue had tears in his eyes when everything burst into flames. Doc's jaw was set with fury. Arky's throat tightened so hard with anger he thought he'd choke.

The men waited till everything had burned to coals. Fong turned and bowed. 'Thank you for your gifts.' He smirked, left the smoking cave and switched on his torch. 'There's a big snowstorm coming,' he called from outside. 'You will not escape again. You are not even worth a bullet. The weather is a pitiless enemy. I think we will never meet again.'

His torchlight faded as he walked away into a whirl of drifting snowflakes.

Escape from Leopard Mountain

'*Now* what?' asked Bear, shivering.

'I'm not sure,' Doc replied, through chattering teeth.

Arky knew that it wouldn't be long before they'd freeze to death.

'We have to find a way to keep warm,' Tue said, as if he could read Arky's thoughts.

'There might be wood in the other caves,' Arky suggested.

'It's dark,' answered Doc, 'but it's worth the hunt.'

'There are embers still glowing on the fire.' Bear

pointed them out. 'We might be able to light it again if we found wood.'

'I'll look,' said Doc. 'You boys stay here. No point in us all freezing outside. Try to find something that'll keep the embers alive till I get back.'

While Doc was gone, the boys searched for where the wood had been stored. Their fingers soon touched splinters and little sticks. They collected them, placed them on the embers and blew gently. A tiny flame spread light.

To Arky's relief, Doc soon returned with an armload of wood. Stick by stick they fed the fire. 'There's lots more wood in the next cave over,' Doc shivered, but he was beginning to sound more cheerful. 'We should move to the wood, rather than go out and back, carrying wood here. Can you boys keep the embers alive on a burning stick?'

The boys nodded. Doc selected larger sticks with glowing coals and handed them to the boys. Naked, they stepped outside, carrying their firesticks. Arky gritted his teeth against the biting snow. It was so dark he had to watch the glowing coals the others carried so he didn't get lost. By the time he reached their destination, his feet were numb and he felt sick with cold.

Once inside, they put their sticks together and made a new fire. As the cavern filled with light, they collected more wood and fed the blaze. Shivering so badly his kneecaps were shaking, Arky looked for something to help him warm up. His eyes soon fell upon a hermit hole. There was an item in it. Curious, he went over and dragged out something that felt like it was made of dusty wool. It was a robe and, as he shook it, a cloud of dust made him sneeze. A long booger of snot fell down his face and he wiped it with the back of his hand. He pulled the robe over his head. Then he noticed a pottery oil lamp in the hole. He took it to the fire. To everyone's delight the grease inside flared. 'Now I have a little lamp,' said Arky. 'I'm going to hunt in the other sleeping nooks for more clothes.'

Leaving the others, he set off on frozen feet. Just as the old lamp's flame guttered, he found a moth-eaten fur cloak and two more robes. He returned to the fire, giving the clothes to Doc to share out.

'If hermits can live wearing these, then so can we,' said Doc, pulling a robe tight around him.

Tue took the fur cloak, turning it inside out so the fur was against his skin. 'Very warm.' He grinned.

'It smells awful.' Bear wrinkled his nose and dragged the dusty robe over his head. 'And it makes me itch!'

Arky was about to thump Bear for being so ungrateful, when Bear burst out laughing. 'Only joking.' He smiled. 'Aren't we lucky you found them? And we have a fire to warm our frozen feet!'

The snow stopped falling in the morning. As the sunlight appeared, they searched the hermit holes for more clothes. Tue found two old blankets. He tore one to shreds, showing Arky and Bear how to bind their feet with the strips to make shoes. 'I didn't always have shoes,' he told them. 'I often had to use old clothes for my feet. And I am very cross I have lost my new boots!'

Doc laughed. 'Tue, when we get back we'll buy you more than just new shoes, but first, let's rip up this other blanket and make gloves and headscarves to protect ourselves for our walk back.'

Once they were wrapped up, Doc said, 'I think we should get back to where the helicopter dropped us as fast as we can.'

With all the drama Arky had almost forgotten the pink carving he had hidden in the cave. He dashed off and brought it back to his father.

'It was in the crown,' he said. 'What does it mean?'

'It's a good luck symbol.' Doc inspected the intricate carving. 'It isn't valuable. It's quartz. There are hundreds like it on the market. Even a very old one only brings a few hundred dollars.'

'Why is it good luck?' Bear asked.

'Well, there's a legend about lucky walnuts,' Doc began.

'I knew you'd have a story.' Bear laughed. 'So go on, tell us while we walk back.'

On the way back down the mountain, Arky noticed that even though his feet were cold, they weren't frozen. Tue's clever shoes stopped his toes from being frostbitten.

After a few hours the clouds closed in and it began to snow again. 'This isn't good,' Bear moaned.

'Try to keep your spirits up,' Doc said.

Bear nodded and, to Arky's surprise, he broke into a loud tune. His voice, clear and bright, echoed loudly through the ravine.

'Stop!' Tue pushed Bear hard in the back as Bear's voice continued to reverberate.

'Why?' asked Bear, shocked by Tue's assault.

'You are shaking the snow!' Tue said as a loud rumbling stopped them in their tracks. A powdery dusting of snow fell onto Arky's shoulders.

'Run!' Tue screamed, but he was too late. With a splintering crash, ice bounced around them, and

Arky looked up to see a massive white wave hurtling down the mountain.

Hundreds of tons of snow tore Arky from the track and flipped him over and over. For a few seconds he bobbed like a cork on the surface of the roaring snow. Large lumps of ice bruised and battered him; snow filled his ears, nose and mouth as he spun wildly out of control.

The speeding snow flipped him high one last time, and the surge that followed it buried him. The world became dark and weight pressed on his chest. He couldn't breathe. He thought of his mum, and how sad she'd be if he and Doc were both killed. As his oxygen ran out, red spots flickered before his eyes. Then, suddenly, the speeding avalanche spat him out and he found himself resting beside a rock. He staggered to his feet, spitting snow from his mouth, retching and gasping for air. The avalanche sped on down the hill, leaving him in its wake.

It took him a while before he could stop his lungs heaving and gather his thoughts. He looked around, desperately searching the snow for any sign of the others. He stumbled towards a dark shape several metres to his left. It was Tue's head. Tue was gasping and muttering in his own language—but at least he was breathing. Further away, Arky saw a pair of feet jutting up into the air. He made a quick decision. He raced to the feet and dug frantically. Luckily, Bear was only just under the surface. Arky pulled his friend free, opened his mouth, stuck his fingers inside and removed the snow. Bear choked and his head shook. Arky breathed a sigh of relief.

As Arky worked to free Bear, Tue struggled out from under the snow and helped. They both studied Bear closely as he gasped and opened his eyes.

'Are you hurt?' Tue asked.

Bear shook his head and shakily rose to his feet.

'Dad?' Arky looked frantically around the slope. 'Dad!'

'He must be buried.' Bear barely had enough breath to speak.

'Search!' ordered Tue, seeing the desperation in Arky's eyes. 'Stamp and call and listen. Sometimes people can be caught in an air pocket. They manage to make air around their heads but are buried. They can hear if you call. If you listen you can hear them call back. Count to five, call and listen. Then repeat. He is heavy so he may be further down from us.'

Arky and Bear followed Tue's command. They spread out and made their way down the slope. Their calls echoed through the valley, until Bear stopped. 'Here,' he cried, 'I think I hear something.' Arky and Tue rushed over.

'Dad!' Arky shouted with all his might.

'Mmmmrph,' came a soft reply. The boys began digging. After a few moments they found Doc, chilled but very much alive.

That night, under a starry sky and a beautiful moon, they huddled together for warmth beneath a rock overhang. Arky dozed off in his father's arms. He woke to find Tue with his head on Doc's lap and Bear tucked up with his head on Arky's shoulder. He looked up at his dad. Doc was smiling at him.

'What a good team we are,' Doc whispered. 'We'll get back to the helicopter easily tomorrow.'

Arky suddenly remembered the carved good luck charm. He patted his pocket. Miraculously, it was still there.

God's Eye

After the helicopter dropped Doc and the boys safely back in Ulaangom and they had recovered from their ordeal on Leopard Mountain, Lord Wright asked them to meet him at a small restaurant near their hotel.

'We have to be careful,' he said. 'It is obvious your hotel rooms are bugged and that Rulec found out what we were up to. He must have taken Fong and this other thug after you in his helicopter. How else could they have found you so quickly? This is why we are meeting here, so we can't be overheard.'

'We thought so,' Doc said. 'We've been very careful since we returned.'

'This terrible ordeal and theft is something we must keep to ourselves,' Lord Wright said, his voice tense. 'It won't do for anyone to know we have lost Genghis Khan's crown and the Hand of Death. It would ruin our reputation and destroy any chance of you finding more work in other countries.'

'That's the end of it then?' asked Doc. 'We stop here?'

'Yes, I believe we should accept our losses,' Lord Wright said. 'We should be happy with the wonders you found in the tomb.'

Arky noticed his dad hadn't mentioned the little carving he had discovered inside the crown. He wondered if he thought so little of it that he'd forgotten it after the avalanche.

Lord Wright turned to the boys. 'You've done a great job, but your part in this adventure is over. I've decided to have Richard fly in and look after you until we leave.'

'Not the butler!' Bear crossed his arms and slouched back in his chair.

Lord Wright ignored Bear. He turned to Tue and patted his shoulder. 'Tue, I'm organising for you and your sister to have scholarships so you can go to school and university. This will be a small reward for everything you have done for your country in helping find the tomb. I hope you will like this.'

Tue beamed. 'My parents will be very proud.'

'Richard will be here in a couple of days,' Lord Wright said, addressing all three boys. 'You can entertain yourselves till then without getting into trouble, I'm sure.'

'Playing computer games in the hotel room,' Bear said. 'Boring!' But Bear looked at Arky with such rebellious eyes that Arky doubted they'd have a dull time while they waited for Richard.

Arky was thoughtfully eating a Mongolian honey and walnut cookie that Tue had bought them to try, when he remembered something important. 'Do you guys remember the story Doc told us?'

'What story?' Tue seemed bewildered by the random question.

'The one about the lucky buddha walnut carving we found in the crown. He told us about it when we walked back from Leopard Mountain.'

'He tells so many stories,' Bear said, 'it's hard to remember. Why do you ask?'

'I think what he told us might help us find the next clue to the treasure,' Arky replied.

'Remind us of the story.' Bear seemed more interested now.

'Doc said it was carved with lots of buddhas to look like a walnut, because the walnut was God's favourite food.' Arky tried to remember the story as accurately as possible. 'The little buddhas are carved in it to remind us that Buddha was reborn on earth 108 times. At the end of Buddha's 108th life, the great God looked at Buddha and was happy with him. "My eye is pleased," he said.'

'People put a third eye in Buddha's forehead to represent God's eye,' added Tue. 'All buddhas have three eyes.'

'If the Buddha had 108 lives and the walnut carving is supposed to represent 108 buddhas, then maybe we should look for something nearby with 108 buddhas, or something with a buddha eye?' Bear was warming to the idea of another quest. 'Let's look on the computer and see if there is anything like that.'

They spent several minutes searching the net for words like '108 buddhas', 'eyes' and 'Mongolia'.

'We're not having much luck,' said Tue.

'Luck?' Arky said, thinking. 'We forgot that the carving we found is lucky. Perhaps we should try words like "lucky", "lucky eye", that sort of thing.'

Bear went back to googling and, after several minutes, he looked up and tipped the screen so Tue and Arky could see what he'd found. 'Look! An old pyramid of buddhas. It's not far from town and it is called "The Shrine of Luck".'

'It couldn't hurt to have a look,' Arky said. 'I wonder how many buddhas are in it?'

'All it says is that it's about nine hundred years old,' Bear said. He brought up a map of the area.

'See, here it is by the river, close to the glacier. It's a few hours' walk at most. We could check it out.

'I'd like to find the treasure before we're sent home,' he continued. 'How about tomorrow we sneak off and—'

'And last time we did that we got kidnapped,' Tue said. 'This would be most unwise. We should always let your father know where we are.'

'But if we go really early,' insisted Bear, 'before breakfast, I think we could walk down to those buddhas. We don't have to tell anyone. We could just go for the day. We're allowed out on our own now. I don't think anyone would miss us.'

Arky surprised himself when he nodded in agreement. He didn't like going behind his dad's back, but the idea of an adventure was too hard to resist.

Both boys looked at Tue. He shrugged his shoulders and held his hands up in the air. 'I give up,' he said. 'I'm with you! We've been lucky so far.'

'Tell your dad you're sleeping in my room tonight,' Bear told Arky, 'so we can leave early in the morning. My stepfather never even checks to see if I'm alive. It'll be easy to bunk off without anyone knowing.'

The boys bought food and prepared their backpacks for the trip. Arky made sure he prepared for any emergency and included torches, bandaids and toilet paper. Bear's credit card got quite a workout.

Early the next day, Tue met Arky and Bear at the back of the hotel. They raced down the street, leaving the main part of town. When they reached some poorer suburbs, a man carting hay stopped and gave them a lift. He turned off near the glacier so the boys got out and thanked him for his help. Then they walked up a narrow road till they came to a cliff. They looked down upon an angry river, tumbling from the glacier. A huge waterfall with clouds of spray glittered with rainbows in the morning light.

Above the rainbows, high on the steep rock face above, sat a crumbling pyramid of buddhas. They were darkened by the long shadows cast from the hills opposite.

The boys clambered up to the first row of buddhas and began counting them, checking each face for an unusual third eye painted on the buddha's brow. All the buddhas held their arms up, supporting the second row of buddhas. The boys climbed up to the next row.

The second level of buddhas had third eyes carved like walnuts sticking out from their brows, but there was nothing unusual. They, in turn, supported a third row of smaller buddhas who had eyes set with coloured granite. The boys climbed upwards, counting—105, 106, 107—to the final buddha at the peak of the pyramid.

'It has a hole in its forehead!' cried Arky excitedly, standing in front of the 108th statue's face. The buddha's head was tilted down so it stared at the raging waterfall. Arky reached into his pocket, removed the carving and popped it into the hole. It fitted perfectly. They waited.

Bear poked it once or twice and finally, disappointed, he pulled it out. 'Nothing!' he moaned. 'Nothing happened.'

'We're missing something,' Tue said.

'What have we missed? Breakfast?' Bear's stomach rumbled loudly.

'Think!' yelled Arky. 'And stop making stupid jokes.'

'Okay . . . There are 108 buddhas here. We got the eye of the Buddha from behind the eyes of a buddha. We could see a long way—'

'One zero eight,' Arky said slowly, interrupting. 'One and zero and eight are nine.'

'What are you getting at?' Bear looked confused.

'I mean, we had 999 dead men in nine rows. We had nine rings of the gong. We had 999 dragons. Every time we had a clue it somehow came back to nine.'

'Every time,' agreed Tue.

'Time! *And in time ye shall name the king*,' Bear quoted from the last story in Tue's book. 'Did people back in Genghis's day know the time?'

'We have always had sun clocks,' replied Tue. 'They knew there are twenty-four hours in the day.'

'Well, what's the time now?' Arky cried. 'The face of the Buddha was in shadow when we first arrived, and now it is almost in the sun.'

'Eight thirty,' said Bear, checking his watch.

'Nine o'clock.' Arky laughed. 'Let's put the walnut back in and wait for nine o'clock!'

In the ninth hour of the day, the sun struck the 108th buddha's eye. It lit the carved ornament like fire. A bright pink ray shone from the buddha's forehead like a search beam, and speared downwards between the sheer cliffs into the waterfall.

'Is the next clue near the waterfall?' Arky wondered.

'Do we have to look?' Tue groaned.

'There are cliffs between us and the waterfall. And at the bottom are dangerous rocks,' Bear said. 'I don't like the look of that!'

'But look further down the river,' said Arky, pointing. 'We can get down there. We could walk down to that river edge and have a look from the bottom.'

The boys kept watching the waterfall until the sun moved and the ray in the eye went out. Arky pulled the walnut jewel from the buddha's head and put it carefully in a zip pocket in his backpack. They began their descent.

'I don't feel so safe!' Bear shouted, over the roar of the waterfall. He had just climbed up to Arky, who had found an old path cut into the rocks.

'This trail is pretty crumbly,' Arky agreed, as spray drenched them. 'If we slip, we're dead meat. We're pretty high up.'

'It was invisible from above,' Bear said. 'I doubt anyone has been here for years. If we fall, our bodies will be carried away and no one will ever find us.'

'If you study the path,' Arky said, trying to ignore their danger, 'it ducks around the corner there.' He pointed to the edge of the thundering curtain of water. 'I think it goes behind the waterfall.'

'I'm not happy about being in dark caves with water again,' Tue said, sounding worried.

Bear took one look back down the river and made up his mind. 'We'll go on for a few more minutes. If it's too tough we'll go home.'

'Are you game to go on, Tue?' Arky asked, pulling the torches from his pack.

Tue shrugged. 'I have gone this far,' he replied. 'I'm not going back without you.'

The boys moved cautiously along the track, watching their feet so they didn't slip. Eventually they found their way into a dry tunnel behind the waterfall.

'I think we're to be congratulated.' Bear smiled as they took out their torches and switched them on. The tunnel was straight and dry and they followed it upwards until the roar of the waterfall faded.

After some fast walking they came to the end of the tunnel. Bear thumped the walls in front of him. 'Seriously disappointing.' He shone his torch up to the roof. 'Oh look! Just to cheer me up, there's a lovely death head staring down and it has a third eye!'

Arky and Tue both moved over and stood beside Bear, shining their torches upwards at the leering skull.

'It's a pink eye,' Arky said.

Then the earth below their feet shook, the ground gave way and the boys were tumbled, screaming, into the dark.

The Cavern of Death

Arky rolled down a steep tunnel. Then he fell through the air and landed heavily on something that knocked the wind out of him. He struggled for breath and tried to sit up. His torch lay beside him, highlighting the skeletal body of a goat. He'd landed on a dead goat! Gasping, he picked up his torch and shone it around. It was like he was at the bottom of a well carved into the rock.

Tue was already standing beside him, shining his torch up at the tunnel they had tumbled through. Arky calculated they had fallen over three metres from the hole above his head. No wonder his breath had been knocked out of him.

Further up from the trapdoor tunnel, about five metres above his head, was the roof. Painted on the roof was a large grinning white skull, with a third eye on its forehead. The third eye shone bright pink under his torchlight. The skull looked like it was laughing at him. *Some joke*, Arky thought.

He turned to check on Bear, who was lying spread-eagled on his tummy, groaning. Beside Bear was another dead goat.

'I'm not opening my eyes,' Bear said, as Arky's light flashed over him. 'Not until one of you tells me we're not trapped and I'm not looking at the horned skull of the devil!'

'You'll be there a long time then,' Tue snapped. 'Because we're stuck in a horrible hole with dead goats.'

'I knew it!' Bear groaned. 'It stinks in here!'

Arky ignored him and continued playing his torch over the smooth circular walls of their prison, looking for an escape. 'What's that?' he asked, as his torch lit a faded painting of a fierce blue god wearing a painted necklace of skulls and holding a sword.

'It is the God of Death.' Tue shivered slightly. 'His name is Yama. This is a bad omen.'

Bear moaned, switched on his torch, rolled over and shone it up at the roof. 'A skull with a pink eye! Oh, that's cheerful! How did we get in here?'

'We must have stood on some sort of animal trap,' Arky explained, glad Bear was coming to his senses. 'I think it was designed to collapse under a certain weight, like the weight of a man. The three of us standing together would have triggered it, and we rolled down a steep tunnel and fell in here.'

Bear stood up and reached for his phone. 'No damn reception,' he bellowed. 'Just when you need it, it doesn't work!'

'There has to be a way out!' Tue used his torch to search the walls again. As his torch flickered over the painted Yama, Arky noticed a shadow.

'There,' he cried, pointing. 'Against the blue god! Is that a lever?'

Bear wasted no time and strode over to the artwork to inspect it closely. 'It looks like a painted sword.' He put his hand on the shadow.

'But . . . You're right! It *is* a lever! I wonder what it does?'

'Don't pull it!' screamed Arky and Tue together.

'Oops,' Bear said. There was a moment of scared silence as they waited to see what Bear had done. Then a grinding noise came from the tunnel they had just fallen down. There was an odd rushing, gurgling sound, and to Arky's horror a fountain of water poured from the tunnel and ran down the wall.

'Push the lever back!' Arky shrieked, above the noise of the spurting water.

Tue and Arky rushed to Bear's side, frantically pushing and pulling, but the lever wouldn't move. The fountain became a spout and the water surged to their waists in minutes. As their hole filled, they were forced to tread water and float.

The grinning skull with the third eye came closer and closer as they bobbed towards the roof.

In a few minutes they would be caught against the ceiling and run out of air. Tue had already slipped under twice and dropped his torch.

'I don't swim very well,' he puffed, struggling, 'so I will say goodbye.'

'We're going to drown,' Bear panted. 'Sorry, guys.'

Arky's heart tightened at his friends' words. He wondered if he should say goodbye too. He shone his torch at Bear, who was wide-eyed with terror and gasping. Through his frightened thoughts, Arky searched desperately for a way out. He shone his torch at the terrible skull. It was so close he could almost touch it. The third eye in its wicked face had pink paint all around it. Then he saw a hole!

The hole was in the black pupil of the third eye. It looked about the same size as the carved walnut.

'Pink!' yelled Arky. 'Quick! Bear, get the lucky charm out of my backpack. Don't drop it! It's pink! We have to put it in that hole.'

As the water brought them face to face with the grinning death head, Arky helped Tue stay afloat while Bear struggled with Arky's backpack. With seconds to spare, he retrieved the carving and jammed the relic into the third eye.

The most satisfying click Arky had ever heard echoed in the small space against the roof.

There was a gurgling, like someone had pulled a bath plug. The water swirled and they were sucked down. Before Arky could think, they were shot through a drain at the bottom of the hole, and spat out with a mighty splash into another room. A stone door slammed hard behind them, the water stopped, and the boys stood shakily.

The Sword of Justice

They were in the base of a bottle-shaped cavern. High above them was a cleft that let in filtered light. In front of them was a statue. 'Yama again!' Arky sighed.

This Yama stood three metres high, and was fat and hideous. His fiery eyes bulged threateningly. His fierce jaws had two long tusks and his long tongue stuck out rudely. Real skulls hung in a necklace around his neck. He pointed a silver sword at a golden cylinder, engraved with dragons, lying at his feet.

Arky grabbed the cylinder. Unscrewing the lid, he pulled out a calfskin scroll. As he carefully unrolled the vellum, a bright and colourful map was revealed.

'Look, there's the Shrine of Luck!' cried Bear, slapping Arky heartily on the back. 'And there's the waterfall!'

The map also showed the glacier. Men were pictured walking up the glacier, lugging packs like the ones yaks carried. Wooden yokes were twisted under their elbows, so the weight of their burden went up onto their shoulders. Their hands were clasped behind their backs.

A rocky, needle-like crag stood out on the map near a big twist in the glacier. Further up from the rocky needle, inside the glacier, was a large circle, painted blue. Inside the circle were golden boxes.

'It's a treasure map! We've found where the treasure is hidden,' Arky said.

'But how do we get out of here?' asked Bear.

Arky rolled the map back up and put it inside its cylinder. The boys studied the slick walls, looking for some sort of escape.

'There's light coming in from above, so we are not far from outside.' Tue sounded as if he was trying to convince himself. 'There will be a way to get out, I'm sure.'

Arky studied the walls of the cavern. 'But there is no way to climb up to the light,' he said. 'There's not even a fingerhold I could use.'

'Everything we've found has had a meaning,' Bear reminded them. 'So look around. There's probably a secret door, like in the tomb. We just need to find a clue.'

'We might need Doc's brains,' said Tue. 'We don't know our history very well.'

'But we found this without grown-ups,' argued Bear. 'We can get out!'

'I'm getting very cold,' said Tue, pulling at his wet clothes, 'and very tired.'

Arky was shivering too. His teeth chattered loudly in the small space. The darkness and the chilling water had sapped the strength from him. The nasty Yama statue wearing a necklace of skulls wasn't helping him feel very good either.

'Death, death, death!' yelled Bear, finally losing it and stamping a foot. 'I hate Genghis Khan!'

'Death!' cried Tue, leaping to his feet. 'Think! In the monks' cemetery, the death heads with the golden eyes helped us find the secret door.' He began frantically patting the walls. Bear leapt to Tue's side, kicking at any crack or jamming his fingernails under anything loose.

Arky paced up and down, trying desperately to think clearly. He knew that being angry or scared wasn't useful. His mother had told him many times that she was often scared when she climbed. Once a rope had broken and she was left hanging over a cliff for a few hours. She said that if you were scared, you should breathe deeply and try to clear your mind of what was frightening you. Arky began to breathe and concentrate on a solution.

His friends were slapping the walls crazily, but Arky had a sudden thought. 'Forget the walls and look at the statue,' he said.

His calm voice stopped the other two. Bear bolted to the statue, clambering up till his face was next to the statue's head. 'It looks pretty normal,' he groaned, balancing on the god's bent elbow.

'What's that hanging around its neck?' asked Tue.

Bear pulled off the haunting necklace and slithered down. He sat on the floor, inspecting every skull. 'Bones,' he said. 'Just bones with teeth! No little hidden keys or anything. We're at a dead end.'

Arky found himself smirking at the pun.

'You try.' Bear tossed aside the clanking skulls. 'See if I've missed anything.'

'You know this god, Tue?' Arky said. 'Is there anything else he does? Does he just kill people?'

'Oh, he doesn't kill,' said Tue. 'He is the God of Death, but also the god that gives us justice.'

'It wouldn't be justice if we died after all we have been through,' Bear said.

'In our culture,' said Arky, studying the sword in Yama's hand, 'we have a Sword of Justice that an angel carries.' He prised the sword from the god's hand. The steel blade was still sharp, almost like it was new. On the hilt was a death head. Arky twisted it, hoping it would come undone. 'It's solid!' he said, scowling.

The boys studied the statue further. Arky pulled and pushed each blue finger in case one of them moved. Sadly they were made of strong metal. Bear tried twisting the hands, but there was no hidden spring or movement. Arky stared at the god's fat blue stomach. It had a big, deep belly button.

It reminded him of a joke his mum had told him when he was little. *Why do I have a belly button?* Arky had asked his mum.

To keep your bum on! She'd laughed.

Arky looked closer at the statue's belly button. It went in a long way, like a keyhole. He poked his finger in. It was really deep! 'This is weird,' he said.

'Keyhole!' shouted Bear, excitedly. 'Where's the key?'

'Every clue we've had since we got in behind the waterfall has been a skull,' said Arky. 'The statue had skulls on its neck. Skulls, skulls!'

'The sword has a skull,' suggested Tue.

'If you look at the sword sideways it could be a key,' Bear said. 'Why would Genghis bother to have the sword in here if it wasn't to be used for something?'

Arky carefully turned the sword around. He inserted the hilt into the big god's tummy. It fitted. He turned the sword. To the boys' amazement the statue spun on its pedestal to reveal a tunnel. There was light at the end. Before Arky left the cave, he removed the sword from the statue's tummy, putting it under his arm. Bear carried the golden cylinder with the map and they ran towards the daylight.

Fong and his men had been shocked when the boys and Doc miraculously returned from Leopard Mountain. Fearing the police would come looking for them, they hid. They would have run for their lives, but Rulec had not yet paid them for their work. They waited nervously to see what would happen.

Eventually, Rulec called a meeting with Fong.

'We've been lucky,' he said. 'Professor Steele is not telling anyone about the crown or the hand. He is also keeping quiet about their ordeal. The police are not hunting you.' Rulec handed Fong several thousand dollars from his desk drawer. 'Here is your payment. I want you to get out of town and keep your mouth shut.'

'Is this all?' Fong said, staring at the money. 'What we brought you was worth millions.'

Rulec's eyes hardened.

Fong trembled under the other man's snake-like gaze.

'What you have brought me is trouble and people who have returned from the dead! You are lucky I don't have you all killed for your failure to leave no traces. So, don't tempt me. Get out of town now! If you don't, your brother will think hell is a good place to be!'

Fong was driving out of town, seething with anger, when he saw three dirty, damp boys walking along the side of the road. He recognised them instantly. They were walking oddly, as if they were trying to hide things under their jackets. His interest intensified.

He turned and followed them at a safe distance. It didn't take long before the wind caught at Arky's coat and Fong glimpsed a sword. Several minutes later, Bear stumbled and fell and a glittering cylinder rolled on the ground.

Fong pulled his car over to the side of the road and watched them trying to hide the treasures under their jackets. *I will watch them for a little while,* he thought. *Perhaps they will pay me better than Rulec.*

The Lost Treasure of Genghis Khan

Late that afternoon, after they returned to the hotel, the boys sat in a noisy corner, making sure no one could overhear them. They studied their wonderful map with great care.

'There's a road that goes up a fair way beside the glacier,' Bear said, comparing the map to a current one on the internet.

'The needle-like crag shown on the map is not far away from the road,' Arky added. 'Wouldn't the Keeper of Secrets be surprised to think a big road was so close now?'

'How about we don't tell anyone about our find,' Bear said. 'Not yet. If no one notices we were gone today, I reckon we could go up there tomorrow. We only need food for one day and our wet weather gear. We could get away as soon as everyone goes to work tomorrow.'

'And we should take the sword,' said Arky. 'It could be needed as a key again.'

Bear nodded in agreement.

'To walk on a glacier,' Tue said, 'we will need special shoes and crampons. There is a store in town that sells these.'

'Not a problem.' Bear smiled. 'We'll meet tomorrow just after nine o'clock, when Doc and my stepfather have gone up to the tomb.'

'And if we find the treasure,' Arky said, 'we'll be forgiven for going behind our parents' backs.'

The following morning, the boys dodged down small alleys until Tue felt it was safe to hail a run-down cab. The driver stared oddly at the boys, but accepted them as passengers. They were soon driving out of town.

'I hope we can get home as easily tonight,' said Arky. 'It's a long way back. Will we ask the driver to come back later and get us?'

'No,' said Bear. 'We don't know how long we'll be. Let's just make the most of our last day of freedom.'

As the glacier loomed closer, Tue ordered the driver to drop them off. They paid him, and made their way in the direction of the needle-like crag.

Soon they were crabbing their way along the glacier's melting face. Pools of water lay on its surface. Pitted holes and deep cracks slowed the boys' way as they edged between the steep mountains on each side. Their new crampons stopped them from slipping, but Arky had to dig his feet into the ice with every step. The crag shown on the map came closer as the sun moved higher.

Arky also found the going difficult because he had to hold onto the sword. After a while he tucked it through his belt, although it still flapped annoyingly against his leg. He slipped often, and the cold crept through his gloved hands, making his fingers tingle.

Near the crag, the glacier swung in a tight loop. As they rounded the corner a crumbling ice cliff loomed high above them and blocked their way forwards. Water flowed from beneath the wall of ice, gurgled into a hole and vanished beneath their feet.

'We'd need climbing gear and ice picks to get up there,' Arky said, feeling disappointed. 'Even then, it would be too dangerous to climb because it's melting.'

'But the map says the treasure is further on!' Bear argued.

'It is hundreds of years since the Khan hid the treasure,' Tue said. 'He wouldn't have thought it would take this long for someone to find all his clues. He probably thought they would be discovered just a few years after his death.'

'Hundreds of years,' said Arky, thoughtfully. 'Glaciers move. Some of them travel one metre a year, others metres a day. The treasure would have travelled down with the glacier. It may be closer than we think.'

'If the glacier has moved fast, the treasure would have been washed into the river,' said Tue.

He and Bear looked around sadly.

'We've got this far,' said Arky. 'I'm not giving up just yet. Let's look around. We might find something washed out of the ice. If we find nothing, then we'll go back and turn our map over to the authorities. They can do the maths, and search later.'

'Let's spread out and look behind the big boulders that have fallen from the mountains,' suggested Bear.

The boys hunted around the ice cliff for clues. Arky had just about given up looking at dirty ice when Tue shouted out. He was nearby, waving frantically. Arky stumbled over to his friend.

Tue pointed to a narrow crevasse in the ice. It was tucked up near the mountain slope. A drizzle of water flowed from its foot. 'The crack goes in behind the rocks a long way,' he said.

Bear joined them and peered inside. 'It looks strong,' he said, inspecting the roof and walls.

He took a step. 'There's plenty of light coming in through the ice above.' He went forwards and disappeared around an icy corner.

Arky took a deep breath and followed him. 'What would be the odds of the ice falling?' he asked Tue, who was behind him.

'Don't talk,' whispered Tue, 'and the odds will be better.'

The boys made their way inside the glacier. Arky had the weirdest feeling, like he was walking through a glass sculpture.

As they moved into the crevasse, the ice trail grew wider, letting in more sunlight. They found themselves in an ice grotto. In front of them was another large cave-like entrance. Bear strode confidently inside and disappeared from sight. Then came a terrified echoing cry.

Arky ran after Bear and found him pointing ahead, his face a picture of disbelief. Arky followed his gaze. Trapped in the ice were men. They wore strong woollen clothes and blood still darkened their chests. Wounds gaped on their heads. Swords, arrows and knives littered the ice near Bear's feet. Old backpacks, like the ones drawn on the map, lay amongst the abandoned weapons.

Arky was so horrified he couldn't move or speak. Skeletons and mummies were one thing, but murdered men who had been preserved in ice for hundreds of years was another.

'We've found it!' Tue said, his breath making a cloud.

With a shudder, Arky turned away from the frozen corpses and looked further into the glassy tomb. The ice cavern in front of him was slippery with melted water. The sunny sky above made everything gleam silver and green. Arky still had shivers down his spine as they moved deeper inside the glacier, and a new sight met his eyes.

Stacked as high as the roof were elephant tusks and bolts of silk encrusted with jewels. Beside them was a tumble of wooden boxes. Some boxes had broken, and bronze and gold coins spilled onto the floor. Emeralds, rubies, sapphires, diamonds and golden necklaces peeked through the sides of rusted iron-bound caskets. Wonderful calfskin-bound books with intricate illustrations lay in piles. There were heaps of rugs, crafted so finely that each one would be worth millions of dollars. There were statues, handcrafted weapons and jade flowers.

It took them several minutes to fully comprehend what lay in front of them. Arky moved over to one of the chests and prised it open.

'So much!' whispered Tue, his voice full of awe. 'My country will not be poor again!'

Bear took a step forward to a large pile of coins tumbling from a box. There was a nasty cracking sound beneath his feet. He looked down. 'The ice is thin,' he said. 'Look, you can see water flowing beneath us. Don't stand together or our weight might break the ice.'

Arky stooped to gather a beautiful jade flower and an emerald brooch. 'It's time to go,' he said. 'We have enough proof that we're not lying about what we've found.'

The words were barely out of his mouth when a noise came from behind them. He turned. Fong and two other men, holding guns, had entered the cavern.

Fong's eyes opened wide as he took in all the treasure in the grotto. He waved his gun and pushed past the boys, reaching for a handful of jewels. The other men also leapt towards the riches.

Realising the men were distracted by the wealth, Arky crept slowly towards the entrance. Bear and Tue followed. They were almost there, when Fong remembered them and turned.

'Stop!' he yelled. 'Back against the wall.' He raised his gun.

'If you fire your gun in here,' shouted Bear, 'you'll make the roof fall on you.'

Fong lowered the gun. His eyes glittered. 'You might be right! Such a helpful boy! Perhaps I will shoot you outside.' He turned to the men, who were filling their pockets with piles of jewels. 'Stop!' he ordered. 'We get rid of the brats now so they can't talk. Then we sort through the treasure. We can come back and back till we are like kings.'

The men turned, grinning at their captives, and moved to stand beside their boss.

'March out of the cave.' Fong waved his gun at the boys and the three men stepped forwards, menacingly.

As they moved, Arky noticed the ice crack under their feet. Fong hadn't realised they were on thin ice. *If only the ice would break*, thought Arky. *If I could make them stand still for just a second . . .*

Then he had a desperate idea. He pulled his silver sword from his belt and waved it through the air.

Fong laughed. 'Are you going to fight me with that?' He scoffed and took a step forward. 'A little skinny boy with a big sword!' The men behind him laughed too.

Arky held the sword high, gripping the hilt with both hands.

'So fierce,' Fong mocked. He levelled his gun at Arky. 'I will take the risk and shoot you here,' he said as Arky stepped forwards. 'So, put the sword down!'

'I will,' shouted Arky, plunging the sword with all his might into the thin ice. The sword went deep.

Before Fong could react, Arky pulled the sword backwards as hard as he could, so it curved under the pressure. Then he let go. The sword twanged back and forth fast. *Whhooka! Whhooka! Whhooka!*

The vibrations from the shimmering sword cracked the ice in front of Arky. The crack shot towards Fong at an alarming rate and he stared at the ice for a second, not understanding what was happening. By the time he realised, it was too late.

The thin ice under Fong's feet split. With a crash, the ice gave way and he fell into the deep icy water beneath. He fired his gun as he went, causing a huge chunk of ice to break off from the ceiling and crash through the thin ice beside him. Falling shards hit the other men and the ice below them shattered. They too sank into the pool.

Their heavy clothes and pockets full of treasure weighed them down and they floundered in the water, dropping their guns.

'Help!' Fong pleaded with the boys. The other men scratched the edge of the ice with their fingers, trying to get out. More ice was breaking.

'We'll fall too if we get too close,' Bear said, watching the ice crack further up into the treasure cave.

'They'll die in a few minutes,' said Tue, sadly. 'The water will suck all their warmth out.'

'We can't let them *die*,' Arky cried. 'We're not monsters.'

'Over there!' Bear pointed to some silk carpets. 'Roll them onto the ice. Then tie some of the ropes lying around together. We can pull the men onto the carpets, and spread their weight. The carpets might hold them on top of the ice.'

The boys set to work. In seconds they had made a platform of carpet. They threw a rope to one of the men. He grabbed it just as his head went under the water. Slowly they hauled him to the surface. He was wet and heavy and it took all three boys to pull him to safety, but he was too exhausted to struggle. Once he was on the carpet, Tue looped a rope around the man's hands and bound them behind his back.

They turned to save the next man, and as he was pulled onto the carpet, Fong sank. He surfaced again, struggling weakly. 'Help,' he whimpered. The boys threw him a rope and hauled him onto the ice.

Finally, they had three shivering captives. Icicles hung from the men's hair and their lips were blue. 'We have to get them moving fast!' said Tue. 'If they sit still they will freeze to death.'

'We'll get them working.' Bear smiled. 'That'll warm them up.' He headed out the entrance and returned with two ancient swords. 'We'll march them home at sword point!' He brandished a sword under Fong's nose. 'Stand up!'

Fong did as he was told. His eyes had lost their aggression and Arky was sure he could hear his bones rattling, as Fong was shaking so hard from the cold.

'I've got another idea,' Arky said, looking at the old packs lying on the floor beside the cavern's entrance. 'We'll get them to do some work. They'll carry a heavy weight so they will need to watch their feet all the way down the glacier. If they fall over, they will not get up again!' He glared at the men. 'You've had your last chance, so do as we say!'

Bear and Tue smiled, understanding what Arky had in mind. They too had seen the map, showing how Genghis's footmen carried the treasure up the glacier like beasts of burden. The boys raced over and picked up three old packs.

Bear pointed his sword at Fong's throat, so he couldn't move. Arky wound the ancient pack onto Fong's back, hooking his elbows with a wooden pole, so the weight went up to his shoulders and his arms remained behind his back, trapped by the wooden pole and bound together. The other bandits were also harnessed in the same way.

Carefully the boys tiptoed around the ice, collecting jewels, necklaces, trinkets, gold and chains. They loaded the men with the treasure. Once the ancient packs looked full, the men were marched out of the cave at sword point.

As they made their slow way down the glacier, Arky saw several people coming towards them. It didn't take him long to recognise Doc, Lord Wright and Is amongst men in uniforms.

'Police!' cried Bear. 'I think we're in trouble.'

Saying Goodbye

The police quickly took charge of the boys' prisoners. Arky wished he'd had a camera so he could have photographed the shocked looks on the policemen's faces when they saw what was in their captives' packs.

'How did you find us?' Tue asked.

'The taxi driver who dropped you off at the glacier recognised you from the papers. He drove up to the tomb to tell us where you had gone,' Doc said.

'He thought you shouldn't be out climbing glaciers with only one young guide,' Is added. 'He also saw these three men following you. He recognised one of them too, but for the wrong reasons. It seems he was robbed a year or two ago and he never forgot the robber's face. He knew you were in trouble so he came and told us.'

'You snuck off.' Doc's voice grew angry. 'You disobeyed me and you could have been killed.'

'But look what we found!' Bear said, gesturing at the treasure. 'You can't be cross with us.'

'We'll discuss this back at the hotel,' Doc said, very firmly.

Bear and Tue hung their heads, but Arky looked up. He caught a flash of laughter in Is's eyes. Doc smiled back at her.

'It's quite a find they have made,' said the policeman in charge. 'We will get the army up here to dig out the rest of the treasure. This is a find that will help our nation!'

Doc's hand came down on Arky's shoulder, giving it a reassuring squeeze. 'You'll be forgiven in time,' he said. 'But don't get too pleased with yourself just now.'

❖

Richard the butler picked the boys up at their hotel and drove them to the airport for the flight to Ulaanbaatar, the capital of Mongolia. Richard was tall and very polite, but he made Bear sit beside him on the plane so he couldn't talk to Tue or Arky. If Bear even wriggled in his seat Richard raised a disapproving eyebrow.

Arky could barely contain his excitement about the forthcoming events. The Mongolian president had organised an official party to celebrate the discovery of the tomb and treasure and everyone was coming. Alice, Arky's mother, had finished her climbing expedition and was flying in from Alaska. Arky couldn't wait to tell her about all their adventures. She'd be so proud of them. Arky knew Bear was surprised that his mother, Linda, was cutting short her film shoot to attend the gala night. She would arrive in the capital in a few days' time. He couldn't wait to meet a real film star.

Tue spent the flight looking as excited as Arky felt, but he was locked in his own thoughts. Lord Wright had told Tue that government officials were going to collect his family from their yurt and bring them to the capital for the party. Arky knew Tue's parents would be very shocked when the officials turned up. They didn't have phones or a television and they wouldn't know about Tue's adventures or his success.

Tue turned suddenly and tapped Arky on the shoulder. 'My parents will meet the president! We will go to a grand party. It is an unheard of honour. I can't believe it.'

'I can't believe it either.' Arky smiled. 'My mum will love meeting all of you.'

Alice arrived soon after they were safely in their hotel rooms. She took one look at Richard's stern face and offered to take charge of the boys. Arky wasn't sure who looked happier—Richard, who was given the rest of the week off, or Bear.

Alice used the time before the ceremony began, and before Doc joined them, to go sightseeing. She took the boys to a beautiful lake nestled in the heart of a mountain and to visit some wonderful rock carvings and several temples in the city.

Tue's family finally arrived and enjoyed being the guests of the government and going to expensive restaurants. To Arky's amusement, they loved using the hotel elevator most of all. They had never been in a lift before, not even Tue's parents.

Every time they went somewhere, Tue's sister rushed to be first in the hotel lift so she could push the buttons. Bear and Arky would get a fit of the giggles as Tue's parents would shout in surprise when they emerged on a new floor. Alice had to ask Tue and his sister to stop pushing every button, as they were upsetting other guests.

Finally, the night of the party arrived. Bear became restless and anxious, as his mother was arriving late and he knew he wouldn't see her till they were actually at the party.

Doc, Lord Wright and Is had flown in by helicopter that afternoon and then everyone had been busy getting ready. Doc and Lord Wright donned smart dinner suits with bow ties.

Alice had bought Bear's and Arky's clothes earlier. They had smart suits, shirts, ties and new shoes. She supervised them dressing and did up Arky's tie and then Bear's. Richard stood impassively by, watching her. Once she finished with Bear, he immediately undid Bear's tie and retied it in a special way. 'It's a Windsor knot,' he informed Alice. 'Gentlemen wear Windsor knots in their ties, but the boys really should have had bow ties for this evening.'

Arky and Bear started laughing as Alice's face went red. 'I had no idea,' she said, blushing. 'I'm better with outdoor clothes.'

Tue's family emerged from their rooms wearing national dress. Arky was really impressed because the sides and top of Tue's head had been shaved, leaving a short forelock in the front and a long lock of hair at the back. He looked just like his dad. He was also wearing a deel, or a kaftan, with a high collar and a wide sash around his waist. It was made of blue silk and Arky thought he looked like he could have walked out of a movie about Genghis Khan. Tue's sister and his mother wore their hair in braids looped over their heads and beautiful headdresses.

Alice wore a long blue dress. A new silver necklace adorned her neck. Arky thought she looked beautiful. Doc's eyes blazed at the sight of her.

They all assembled in the foyer waiting for the official cars and Is joined them, wearing a black dress with sparkles around the hem. Everyone's eyes glittered with pride and joy. They couldn't wait to clamber into the cars and get to the celebration.

The summer palace twinkled with lights and people clapped as they arrived. Soon officials whisked Doc and Lord Wright away and Arky and Bear were left to enjoy themselves. They grabbed food from the plates of passing waiters and enjoyed the band playing outside in the courtyard.

There were so many important guests, Arky found it impossible to move. Reporters and photographers were amongst the crowd. The abbot of the monastery where the tomb was found was having his photo taken with the Mongolian president. Tue's father and mother stood behind the president, staring in wonder at all the activity. They had officially presented Genghis Khan's book to the president the day before, and were amazed when he'd appointed them Treasured Tomb Guardians, which came with an income for life.

'What a party!' cried Tue, his face flushed with pride. A medal from the Mongolian president hung from his neck.

Doc was holding Arky's mum's hand. She was so proud and happy.

Is was talking to the governor, who had given her a job as curator of the Ulaanbaatar Museum. She was now in charge of taking some of the tomb's treasures on a worldwide tour, starting in America.

Bear's mother arrived in a flurry of photographs, several minutes late. She had turned up in a private plane, along with her own press team. She wore a gold designer gown. Her smile was fixed, so the cameras would take a good shot. She clutched a giant toy panda bear and rushed over to Bear, thrusting the toy into his arms and hugging him for the cameras.

Bear gave Arky a look that showed his disappointment. Lord Wright joined his wife's side as Linda proudly dragged Bear towards the president. The glare of flashlights was blinding.

'Incredible,' muttered Arky, taking another nibble from a passing tray.

'I feel sorry for Bear,' Tue said. 'His mother doesn't really understand him.'

'Or even know how old he is,' agreed Arky. 'A panda bear!'

'Doesn't the press love her!' Doc said, his eyes disapproving. 'Poor Bear looks like he wants the floor to cave in.'

Alice looked irritated. 'Poor Bear,' she said. Her brow furrowed, then she leant over and whispered in Doc's ear.

'I'll talk to Lord Wright,' Doc said. He left Arky and Alice and went in search of his friend.

Arky knew he should feel happy about all their success but suddenly he felt sad. After this party, everyone was going home. Bear was off to boarding school in Switzerland. Tue was staying in the capital, a long way from his yurt, and Arky would go home. He vaguely looked forward to being with his friends, but school would seem very dull after all their adventures.

Bear finally broke free from his mother and joined Arky and Tue, carrying a package under his arm. 'I have to say goodbye now,' he said. 'My mother's taking me back to her hotel. We're flying out tomorrow.' He held out the package to Tue. 'I know you'll be busy with school and your family, so I hope you'll accept this gift. It is a computer. It has a camera and you'll have internet at your school. You can talk to me or Arky any time and we can see each other on the screen, like on TV.'

Tue took the package and smiled. 'I would like to see you.' He bowed. 'I think we should never lose touch.' He put the computer down, reached out and hugged Bear.

As Bear was saying goodbye to Arky, Doc and Alice came over. Doc put his hand on Bear's shoulder.

Tue bowed to them, grinning from ear to ear. 'I have a computer!' he said. 'I never thought I'd own such a thing. My friend Bear has given it to me!'

'I guess we'll stay in touch,' Bear said, sounding glum. He turned to Doc and Arky. 'I hope you'll talk to me too. I'll miss you both.'

Before Arky could answer, Alice interrupted. 'Bear,' she said, 'we know you don't want to go to that school in Switzerland. Doc thinks Arky will miss you too.'

Arky nodded.

'Can't be helped.' Bear shrugged.

'Yes it can,' Alice said. 'We asked Lord Wright and your mother if you could go to another boarding school. There's one near our town, Badger's End. It might not be as posh as you are used to, but it's about half an hour's drive away from us and a good school.'

'It means you can come and stay with us during the school holidays,' Arky broke in, realising what his parents had in mind. 'Or, if you want, even weekends.'

'I'd love that!' Bear was obviously surprised by the offer, but happy too.

'And next school holidays,' added Doc, 'Lord Wright has offered me a job working with a museum in Central America. I'm going to be working on some Aztec sacred wells. The museum there has no money for research so your stepfather is funding it. Alice would like to bring you over when I finish up, and we can travel as *real* tourists and see some Aztec and Toltec ruins. Would you enjoy that?'

A smile split Arky's face. 'I would!' he cried. 'Aztecs! They cut people's hearts out.'

Bear turned to Arky. 'Did they?'

'And they threw people into volcanoes, and gold into wells—and everything!' Arky was thrilled to be thinking about their next adventure.

❖

While Arky was at the celebrations in the Mongolian capital, Rulec was back in his mansion, standing before the Crown of Genghis Khan and the Hand of Death. They sat side-by-side in a glittering silver case.

He picked up the hand and put it on a marble table. He admired the beautiful detail of the sculpture, the fine carving on the nails and skin. He spun the hand. It twirled on its support, glittering menacingly. The finger stopped, pointing towards nothing.

'Doctor Steele, may you always have a traitor nearby,' Rulec cursed. 'You are good at your job, but now that you're working for Lord Wright, I will be keeping an eye on you.'

KEEP READING FOR A SNEEK PEEK OF

ARKY'S NEXT ADVENTURE . . .

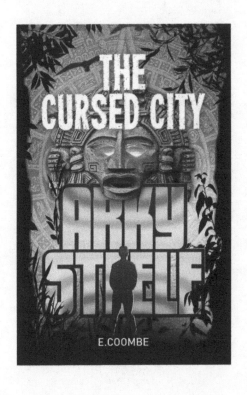

THE CURSED CITY

ARKY STEELE

E.COOMBE

Danger at the Sacred Well

Arky led Bear and Mia back along the waterfall track. They stopped to get their breath at a rocky outcrop that gave them a clear view down through the trees to their campsite. The Sacred Well glimmered sapphire blue in the morning sunlight, a bright contrast against the heavy green jungle.

Their tents were erected in a clearing, serviced by a rough, rutted bush road. A truck was parked beside the mess tent. Camilla, Mia's mother, was preparing the breakfast dishes. Her bright red bandana and long heavy skirt were different from the blue jeans and yellow shirt Alice, Arky's mum, wore.

Alice, her long dark hair shining in the sunlight, was carrying wrapped artefacts to a large packing box. Pancho and Doc stood behind the truck sorting their diving gear and getting ready to pack up and leave. Doc's slightly stooped, well-muscled body made him appear small compared to Pancho's massive shoulders and strong chest.

'My mother is sad you are going,' Mia said. 'This is the only job she gets.'

'Where's your father?' Arky asked.

'Dead.' Mia didn't seem too concerned. 'When I was a baby.'

'Is your village far?' Arky asked, but he was watching the activity below.

'Many hours' drive in your truck. Pancho will take us home later today. I will not see you tomorrow. Can you play baseball with me before you go?'

Arky nodded. 'We'll play this afternoon. Once the work is done.'

'Who's that?' said Bear, pointing. A bare-chested man with long braided hair suddenly emerged from the dense forest near the campsite below, carrying a large machete.

Mia gave a cry of fear. 'Suarez!' She ducked behind a tree. 'Hide! Hide!'

Before the boys could ask why she was so frightened, three men carrying guns erupted from the trees behind the newcomer. A shot reverberated through the air. Pancho dropped what he was doing, spun around and, seeing the invaders, held up his hands. Doc ducked behind the truck, but a fifth man emerged from the trees almost beside him, gun levelled. Doc was captured in an instant.

Alice, seeing the bandits, turned and ran towards the jungle, but another shot rang out. Arky's heart raced hard as a bullet raised the earth near her feet. Camilla screamed and Alice stopped in her tracks. She turned to see Suarez holding his machete against Camilla's throat. Suarez beckoned Alice to return and stand beside Camilla.

Arky wanted to race down and free his parents but Bear had pulled him down behind some bushes. Mia was white with fear.

Once they had their hostages under control, Suarez made the women unpack the box of artefacts. He held each item up for inspection. The jade and gold treasures seemed to cheer him, and a few of them made him slap his thigh with pleasure. Then he passed the best ones around to his men for inspection.

'How do you know this Suarez?' Bear asked Mia, keeping low behind the bushes, but not taking his eyes from the terrible scene below.

'They came to our village,' Mia said. 'Our church had many old paintings and golden icons. Then one day, my mother and I were cleaning the church. This was my mother's job. Suarez came with bandits. He made us lie down. He shot the priest in the leg and stole everything. Now our village is poor. There are no jobs. No tourists come to see the paintings. Our priest had to go to hospital and never came back.'

Once the artefacts had been checked, Suarez ordered his bandits to go through the tents, looking for phones and other valuable possessions. They made a pile of phones, put them in bags and tossed them into the Sacred Well. Then Pancho and Doc were ordered to take down the tents.

'They are going to steal everything!' Bear said as the prisoners dismantled the campsite.

Arky noticed that his parents and Camilla never looked around for him, Bear or Mia. He knew the adults would be hoping they had heard the shots and had the sense to stay hidden.

'The bandits don't know we're here,' he said. 'They're not looking for us.'

'What can we do?' Bear asked.

'Watch and wait.' Arky kept an eye on Suarez. 'Our parents would be more worried if we were captured.'

Suarez made the women repack the artefacts and load them into the truck. Then the bandits filled the truck with tents, tables, chairs, suitcases and anything useful.

When the truck was jam-packed, one of the bandits squeezed into the driver's seat and drove the laden vehicle away.

Suarez and the other bandits pointed their guns at the hostages and marched them into the forest.

'He's taking them!' cried Arky, horrified to see Alice and Doc disappearing into the trees. 'Where's he taking them? Why?'

'Your family is rich,' Mia said to Bear, her voice shaking. 'Everyone knows that. I think it is for ransom.'

'Then why take your mother and Pancho?' Bear asked, but his voice rose in fear.

'If the ransom is not paid, they shoot my mother first to show they mean the business.' Mia sobbed. 'And Pancho is studying at a university so he must be rich too. They will get a ransom for him.'

Arky felt sick. 'We have to do something!'

'We can go and get help,' Bear suggested.

'It's a day's drive to the nearest village!' Arky yelled. 'The trip up here was just forest and more forest. It'd take us forever to walk out!'

'These bad men hide in the jungle so the police can't find them,' Mia said quietly. 'We must follow and find their hiding place. Then we save my mother.'

'Where did the truck go then?' Bear asked.

'I think the truck will go somewhere like a barn, and they will hide the treasures. Then they sell them bit by bit, so no one knows where they came from. But our parents, they will be hidden in the jungle away from a road. Somewhere hard to find.'

'What if Rulec found out about the Spanish Diary?' Arky asked. 'What if he's behind this and wants Dad's computer?'

'If he got the diary, then he might not let them go,' Bear said, his voice on the edge of panic. 'He's tried to kill us before. Maybe he'll get this bandit to hold them hostage and get the information out of them.'

'Mia's right. We have to follow,' Arky said, standing up from behind the bushes. 'We have to save our parents.'

Jungle Horrors

After the sound of Suarez's machete hacking at the jungle had faded, the children crept down into the deserted camp. A broken chair lay against a tree, plastic bags flapped in a light breeze and several food items lay scattered in the dirt.

Arky remembered that Doc and Pancho had stowed some gear down by the Sacred Well. He raced to see if anything was still there, and was rewarded with their backpack, a first aid kit and a knife.

Back at the camp, Bear and Mia rescued a crushed packet of biscuits, a squeeze-bottle full of honey, several tins of fruit and an open packet of tortillas. Bear also found a small plastic sachet with Spanish writing on the label. It looked like raspberry jam so he put it in his pocket.

Arky found two little candles and a lighter. Mia found a tin-opener, a plastic plate, two spoons and some empty plastic bottles. Arky took the bottles and started to head for the well to fill them with water.

'Rainwater only!' Mia yelled out.

Arky sighed. 'We'll need water,' he said. 'It's so hot in the jungle and it's still only morning.'

'Fruit from the tins only,' Mia insisted. 'The well water makes you poo.'

Arky nodded, realising that Mia was most likely right, and threw the bottles away.

When their meagre supplies were packed, Arky shouldered the backpack and the trio headed towards the forbidding jungle. Because Arky had read books his teacher had lent him about Central America's wildlife, he worried about how they would cope with biting insects and wild animals.

Their clothes and shoes were not designed for a jungle trek. And what chance did they have with a little girl in tow? Arky also wished he had a plan. What would they do, even if they did find their parents? He sighed loudly. 'They've got about a half-hour's head start,' he said. 'Mia, you will have to keep up. We can't afford for you to slow us down'.

Mia's dark eyes flashed with annoyance. 'I live here. I can keep up with you!' She tucked her skirt into her undies and strode out after them.

For a while they made good time following the bandits' trail, looking for places where the machete had hewn down a branch or cut away bushes. Towards noon, the jungle opened out and there were no more machete cuts, so they had to search the ground, looking for footprints.

'I'm tired and hot and the jungle is awful and we'll never find them,' Bear grumbled as he searched. He continued complaining and Arky smiled, knowing his friend was quick to grumble but usually meant well.

Mia, however, was not so happy with Bear. She strode up to him and poked him in the chest. 'You are a big scaredy-cat!'

'I'm not!' Bear huffed, blushing at her assault.

Arky was about to stop her from saying anything else when he noticed something glittering at her feet.

'Stop arguing and look,' he shouted, diving on a silver coin, gleaming in the leaf litter. 'Someone's leaving clues. Keep your eyes open and work together.'

The find refocused them and they moved on, Bear discovering another coin and then Mia, a button from a shirt.

'I think the hostages are leaving a trail,' Arky said, as he noticed a bent stick then a scratch on a tree.

By afternoon, tired and hot, Arky called a halt. Mia had tears in her eyes so Arky smiled warmly at her and offered her the first share of biscuits from the pack. Bear opened up a tin of fruit. Arky slurped down his ration and noticed Bear was looking at Mia with what looked like deep respect. He had to admit he admired her too. Not only had she stopped Bear's habit of grumbling, she was strong and had kept up with Arky and Bear, and *she* hadn't complained once.

But then Arky realised that Bear was staring at Mia with a strange intensity. Something was wrong. Arky directed his gaze at Mia, almost jumping in horror. A large black slimy lump was growing behind her ear.

Mia noticed their gaze. 'What?' she asked.

Arky didn't want to frighten her. 'Do you know what is black and slimy and might hang off people's skin?' he asked, trying to broach the subject delicately.

'You found it then?' Mia smiled, and stared at Bear. 'I didn't want Bear to scream.'

'What is it?' Bear was amazed that Mia could be so brave. 'Does it kill you?'

Mia shook her head. 'No, it only sucks your blood. It is a leech. You should not worry, Bear. I can pull the one on the back of your neck off.'

'Back of *my* neck?' Bear squealed, leaping to his feet and slapping at his neck. His fingers found the hideous worm and he let out a yelp and shuddered.

Mia calmly reached over, pulled the leech off and stomped it into the ground. There was a sickening pop as the blood-laden creature burst.

Blood trickled down the back of Bear's neck. Dismayed by the flow, he paled and clamped his hand over the wound. Blood ran down his arm.

'The leech put something in your blood that makes it run for a long time,' Mia explained. 'You'll be all right soon. Just looks bad.'

'Mia, you have one behind your ear,' Arky said, feeling a bit sick.

'Me?' Mia said. 'Why didn't you say so?' She lifted her hand, found the leech, gritted her teeth and pulled hard. The leech flew from her fingers into the bush and her neck ran red, staining her white shirt.

'It looks like vampires have had a go at you both.' Arky shuddered.

'Vampires come at night,' Mia said, in a matter-of-fact voice. 'We are wasting time. We must move.'

'She's my hero,' Bear whispered as Mia marched behind them.

The jungle trail became steep and slippery with mud. Terrible prickle bushes tore at Arky's clothes, and Bear's arms were scratched. But the bushes also made it easier to follow a trail of machete chops and remnants of the hostages' clothing.

In the heat of the jungle, sweat poured from Arky's body. He could see Mia and Bear were suffering too. He knew they had to keep their fluids up. He made the other two stop and he opened the last of the fruit tins. While they sucked down the juice, Arky studied Bear's concerned face. He could see Mia was worried about her mother too. *I hope we haven't made a terrible mistake coming into the jungle,* he thought. *If we don't find our parents, how will we find our way back to camp*? 'We better press on,' he said, trying to look cheerful.

Late in the afternoon, Bear found Camilla's red bandana hanging on a tree. Then their hearts leapt with hope; they could hear a song playing on a radio. Someone was nearby. They crept forward warily, until they spied a clearing with two huts and a large rainwater tank. They'd found the bandits.